ELFIE UNPERFECT

ALSO BY KRISTIN MAHONEY

Annie's Life in Lists

The 47 People You'll Meet in Middle School

ELFIE **UN**PERFECT

KRISTIN MAHONEY

Alfred A. Knopf
New York

THIS IS A BORZOI BOOK PUBLISHED BY ALFRED A. KNOPF

This is a work of fiction. Names, characters, places, and incidents either are the product of the author's imagination or are used fictitiously. Any resemblance to actual persons, living or dead, events, or locales is entirely coincidental.

Text copyright © 2021 by Kristin Mahoney
Jacket art and interior illustrations copyright © 2021 by Dan Santat

All rights reserved. Published in the United States by Alfred A. Knopf, an imprint of Random House Children's Books, a division of Penguin Random House LLC, New York.

Knopf, Borzoi Books, and the colophon are registered trademarks of Penguin Random House LLC.

Visit us on the Web! rhcbooks.com

Educators and librarians, for a variety of teaching tools, visit us at RHTeachersLibrarians.com

Library of Congress Cataloging-in-Publication Data is available upon request.
ISBN 978-0-593-17582-8 (trade) — ISBN 978-0-593-17583-5 (lib. bdg.) — ISBN 978-0-593-17584-2 (ebook)

The text of this book is set in 12-point Adobe Caslon.

Printed in the United States of America
August 2021
10 9 8 7 6 5 4 3 2 1

First Edition

For Whelan, who brings
magic to an unperfect world

CHAPTER 1

I don't know why people think goodbyes are hard. I had to say a whole lot of goodbyes on my last day of fourth grade back in June, and it was easy.

The reason I had to say so many goodbyes was that I was not planning to return to Cottonwood Elementary for fifth grade. Instead, I would be at Hampshire Academy, a private school two towns away. Cottonwood Elementary is a regular, everyday, boring public school. Hampshire Academy is (as I learned on their website) "an Institution with a Tradition of Honor and Excellence."

And the reason it was easy to say so many goodbyes at Cottonwood is that I was happy to leave. Even though I had been there since kindergarten, I had never exactly fit in. I *tried* to fit in. I raised my hand to help my classmates when they gave wrong answers. I offered to take the lead on all group projects and shared all my best ideas. And when I noticed that the cafeteria was particularly noisy at lunchtime, I tried to start a Student Lunch Monitor program.

But it turned out no one else wanted to be a student lunch monitor. It was just Assistant Principal Eastman and me, reminding kids to use their inside voices and throw away their food wrappers. Assistant Principal Eastman asked if I wanted to stop the program and let her handle it with the cafeteria staff, but I said no, I would soldier on. It was an important effort. (Besides, as long as I was working as a monitor, I could eat my lunch standing up, and I didn't have to worry about finding a place to sit each day.)

So my life at Cottonwood Elementary School had been far from perfect. None of the other kids shared my priorities.

Even the one kid at Cottonwood who had known me the longest didn't understand me at all. That would be my cousin, Jenna, who was seven weeks younger than me, lived one mile away, and was about as different from me as a person could be. Jenna was not very interested in schoolwork, or peaceful lunchtimes, or science. She *was* very interested in talking with her friends during school, talking about her friends after school, and planning what she was going to do with her friends on weekends. Jenna had a lot of friends.

Jenna's dad, my uncle Rex, was my mom's brother. Uncle Rex and Jenna came over to our house a lot, especially when Aunt Stephanie, Jenna's mom, was traveling for work.

I guess I should say Jenna *used to* come over a lot. Now

when Uncle Rex comes over, Jenna usually goes to Esme Carter's house, or to the house of one of her other friends. That was fine with me.

Being forced to spend time with Jenna at home was bad enough, but she was also in my class at school last year, and that was even worse. Particularly when we had to do group projects together. *Shudder.*

But that was all going to change tomorrow. Tomorrow I was starting at Hampshire Academy, where I was sure the cafeteria would be peaceful, the other students would be focused on academic success, and the group projects would go just as I wanted them to. (Maybe there wouldn't even be group projects at all! That would *really* be excellent.)

Life at Hampshire Academy was going to be perfect.

It had to be.

CHAPTER 2

Mom and Dad got home from work at around the same time that night. It was our tradition on the last night of summer vacation to go for a special pancake dinner at my favorite restaurant, Mugsy's.

I wanted Rhoda, my babysitter, to go with us. Rhoda has taken care of me since I was a few months old. She is truly one of the greatest people in the world.

But when I asked her to come along, she said she couldn't because she had to study. Rhoda started nursing school this year, and it seemed to be taking a lot of her time. A year ago, she never would have turned down a Mugsy's pancake dinner, but now she had other things on her mind.

Mom gave Rhoda a sympathetic nod when she explained that she had a biology exam the next day.

"I hope you can get some rest tonight," Mom said. "You look exhausted. And pale."

"Oh, I'm just a big ball of stress lately," Rhoda said. "This bio class is kicking my butt."

Mom told Rhoda she should go straight to bed when she got home. Rhoda laughed and said maybe she'd sleep when nursing school was over.

Once we were settled into a booth at Mugsy's, I ordered my usual: chocolate chip pancakes. Mom and Dad got blueberry.

While we waited for our food, I asked Mom and Dad about something that had been bugging me. "Why does Rhoda have to go to nursing school? She already has a great job working for us."

"Well, Elf, we won't need a sitter for you forever," Mom said. "Besides, this is something Rhoda has wanted for a long time."

"How long?" I asked. I mean, Rhoda has been my babysitter for ages; she's really like my third parent. Has she been secretly wanting another job this whole time?

"Well, she first mentioned it years ago, when you were in kindergarten," Mom said. "That was when you were running to try to get a look at a meteor shower and banged your head on your telescope. Rhoda was so good at getting the bleeding to stop right away. When I complimented her on that, she said she's always been good in emergencies, and she'd often thought of becoming a nurse."

"I never knew that."

"Sure you did," Mom argued. "We talk about that telescope story all the time. We were surprised you didn't get a scar." She slid my bangs away from my face so she could touch the spot above my right eyebrow where the cut had been.

"No, I know *that* story," I said, brushing her hand away. "I just never knew the part about Rhoda wanting to be a nurse."

"I could have sworn you knew." Mom was quiet for a second. "You know, even if Rhoda stops sitting for us, she can still visit. She won't become a stranger."

"Yeah, but that's not the same. The setup we have now is perfect."

"Well, Elf, as I've said many times before . . ."

"I know, I know." I rolled my eyes. "Life can't always be perfect."

Dad tried to change the subject.

"So, first day of Hampshire Academy tomorrow! Are you all ready?"

This was a ridiculous question. Of course I was ready. I'd been ready for weeks.

"Totally ready," I said. I held up my fingers one by one and ticked off all the things I'd done. "My pencils are sharpened; they're in my backpack with my pens and my notebook and my calculator. I also packed seaweed crisps for a healthy snack. My uniform is hanging in the front of my closet."

"Well, you definitely sound ready to get out the door,"

Mom said. "But are you feeling nervous about meeting everyone once you're there?"

"Not really." I shrugged.

"Okay. I just know that making new friends isn't always easy for you. I wondered if you wanted to talk about that part of it at all."

"I don't really care about that," I explained. "Besides, making friends wasn't easy at Cottonwood because no one there was like me. That'll be different at Hampshire."

I saw Mom and Dad exchange a look. I know they worry about me not having friends. But I knew I would meet other kids at Hampshire who were serious about learning. And Honor. And Excellence. I was counting on it.

CHAPTER 3

I wanted to go to bed early that night. I needed things to be perfect for the next morning, so I set two alarms: my regular one on my bedside table and a backup clock in the hallway, just in case. I was not going to risk being late for my first day at Hampshire Academy.

But bedtime did not go according to plan. I was in bed by nine, but I could not fall asleep. This was due to the following factors:

- The appearance of a gigantic insect on the ceiling above my bed
- The surge of energy I experienced when I leapt out of bed and hollered for Dad to come get the bug
- The debate that ensued when Dad incorrectly identified the insect as a millipede

Dad insisted that it was a millipede because it looked like it had a million legs. I explained that the prefix *milli-* actually means "one thousand," not "one million." And how even that is a misnomer because millipedes really only have 750 legs, at most. But that didn't matter because the insect on my ceiling was really a *Scutigera coleoptrata*, better known as a common house centipede. Also a misnomer, because they have only 30 legs, not 100, as the prefix *centi-* would suggest. I told Dad that since he was a librarian with easy access to many reference materials, I would think he would know these things.

Dad asked if I wanted him to kill the bug or take notes on my lecture. I told him I hoped he could catch the *Scutigera coleoptrata* in a cup and release it outside, where it might make itself useful eating cockroaches. Dad grabbed a sneaker, stood on my bed, and squashed it instead. "Sorry, Elf," he said. "I'm just not up for a bug chase tonight." I told him he really would be sorry when the next bug we saw was a cockroach.

After the *Scutigera coleoptrata* incident, I was wide awake, wondering how my first day at Hampshire Academy would go. I had toured the school, but I didn't know a single student or teacher there. What would the other kids be like? Would they talk to me? Would there be assigned seats? Would the teachers be different from the teachers at Cottonwood? Would I get lost? (My sense of direction is not my strongest asset.) It was a weird feeling, having a long list of questions that would be answered in a very short time. I reviewed state capitals in a whisper to try to fall asleep.

Mom must have heard me, because she poked her head into my room right after I said "Kansas: Topeka."

"Having a hard time falling asleep?" she asked.

"A little," I admitted. "I'm doing the capitals."

"I heard." Mom smiled. "I hope you can nod off soon. And don't worry, Elf. You're going to have a great day."

• • •

Mom turned out to be wrong. I did not have a great day. It was actually the worst day ever. In fact, my day was so terrible that as a result, I would not be attending Hampshire Academy the following year. Or ever. I was expelled the same day I started.

CHAPTER 4

I t all happened so fast.

Things got off to a good start. I managed to wake up early despite the *Scutigera coleoptrata* incident of the night before, and Dad and I got out the door on time.

When Dad pulled the car into the circular drive at Hampshire Academy, a peppy student with a clipboard and a name tag that said "Zach, Welcoming Committee" opened my car door.

"Welcome to Hampshire Academy!" he said, shutting the door behind me after I stepped out. It was clear that they didn't want parents to wait around. Dad barely had time to get out a quick "Good luck, Elf!" before the door closed.

"Okay . . . name please?" Welcoming Zach asked, looking at his clipboard as I said, "Elfie Oster."

He seemed excited when he found my name.

"Ah, a newbie!" he exclaimed, flipping to the last page on

his clipboard, which was a sheet of what looked like baby bird stickers.

Zach peeled off a sticker and handed it to me.

"This is for all the new students," he said. "Put it on your shirt so everyone will know."

I wasn't sure I wanted "everyone" to know at a glance that I was a new student. But I also didn't want to start my first day at Hampshire by not following directions. I put the sticker on my shirt, glancing around to see if any other kids were wearing stickers. They weren't.

Zach pointed toward the front doors of the building. "Okay, go through there and follow the crowds to the door on your left. That'll be the auditorium. You can find a seat inside for the welcome assembly."

The first thing that felt different about Hampshire Academy was the whoosh of cool air that hit my face as I opened the front door. (Cottonwood Elementary School just had ceiling fans, not air-conditioning.)

The second big difference was the auditorium. Cottonwood's auditorium was plain and brightly lit. The only decorations were the felt banners made by second-grade art classes every fall, and by the end of the year, their letters were falling off, so they said things like "We ove Schoo" and "elcom to Cottonwoo." The seats were lumpy, with uncomfortable springs that poked you if you sat the wrong way. Silver duct tape covered the tears in their scratchy blue fabric.

But the Hampshire auditorium felt like a theater. It reminded me of the symphony hall in Greenville where we went to see *The Nutcracker* last December. There were no bright lights or felt banners, but there was a large crystal chandelier, vines and flowers carved into the wooden trim on the walls, and smooth velvet seats (not a scrap of duct tape in sight).

Most kids were sitting toward the back, talking to their friends. I took an aisle seat in the second row; I figured I should sit near the front so I wouldn't miss any important details. (I almost sat in the first row, then I thought maybe those seats should be saved for visiting dignitaries. Or at least for teachers.)

A tall, thin man with dark gray hair stepped up to the stage. I knew who he was: Headmaster Mulligan. His picture was on the school website, and I had caught a glimpse of him when I visited the admissions office in February for my interview.

Headmaster Mulligan started by saying he wasn't going to give a big speech, but then he talked for a pretty long time, mostly about how Hampshire Academy is a place of Honor and Excellence. He talked a *lot* about the school honor code and how important it was, and how there was a zero-tolerance policy toward honor code violations, and anyone caught cheating or stealing would be expelled immediately.

It all sounded perfect to me. I even wondered if I might

get some kind of Honor and Excellence award at the end of the year.

When Headmaster Mulligan finally finished his speech, Zach and the other welcome volunteers led all the students out of the auditorium and told us to find the classrooms we'd been assigned in our welcome packets. To my relief, my room, number 128, was just down the hall from the auditorium and easy to find.

Inside room 128, I saw "Elfie Oster" written on a paper falcon taped to a table at the back of the room, so I sat there, between a girl (also wearing a baby bird sticker) whose falcon said "Sierra Nichols" and a boy whose falcon said "Colton Palmer."

"Hey," Sierra said, looking at my sticker. "You're new too?"

"Yes. I mean, I was here for my tour, of course. But I've never gone to school here before."

Sierra smiled. "Glad I'm not the only one. This is a cool room, huh?"

I nodded. This room was nothing like Ms. Puckett's classroom, or any of the classrooms at Cottonwood. Hampshire Academy was a really old school, but almost everything in it was brand-new. The desks, the chairs, the shiny floors, the sofa and rug in the meeting area: they all looked like they belonged in a magazine called *Prestigious Academy Living*. On a side counter I noticed microscopes and test tubes that also looked shiny and new. Even the emergency eyewash station looked state-of-the-art. It was heaven.

A woman with chin-length brown hair and metal-framed glasses walked in and stood at the front of the room. I assumed she was our teacher because she was wearing a Hampshire Falcons shirt.

She tapped the Smart Board, and this sign came up:

Good morning, Hampshire Academy!
Welcome to fifth grade!
—Olivia McKee
P.S. A special welcome to our two Eyasses, Elfie and Sierra!

Sierra leaned toward me without taking her eyes off the teacher. "Is she calling us asses?" she whispered. I didn't know what to say. It sort of seemed that way.

Colton Palmer leaned toward us both. "It says '*Ey*asses,'" he said, as though that was much better. "It's what baby falcons are called," he explained.

"Ohhh," said Sierra. She wrote "eyasses = baby falcons" in her notebook. I did the same.

The teacher smiled. "Colton, can you share what you just said with the whole group? It's a good reminder for anyone who hasn't had an Eyass in their class in a while."

Colton stood up. "Okay. That word on Olivia's sign—

Eyasses—means 'baby falcons.' It's what kids who are new to Hampshire are called. Since falcons are our mascot."

I had so many questions. If Colton was calling this woman Olivia (and not Ms. McKee), was she not the teacher? And how did they seem so familiar with each other already, on the first day of school? I was about to learn a few surprising things about Hampshire Academy.

CHAPTER 5

After Colton told us what eyasses are, the teacher said, "I'm Olivia McKee, and I'll be your homeroom teacher this year. I also teach science. You'll go to different classes for math, social studies, and language arts." She looked directly at Sierra and me and added, "Please call me Olivia; all teachers here go by their first names."

Whoa. I'd never heard of that before. I couldn't imagine calling a teacher by her first name; it felt super weird. I didn't even *know* the first names of most of my teachers at Cottonwood.

"A lot of what we do at Hampshire is collaborative learning, meaning we work together to discover things as a group," Ms. Mc—I mean, *Olivia* said. "We're going to do a fun group project today to kick off our year of scientific discovery."

Based on my experiences at Cottonwood, I would never have put the word *fun* with *group project*. I would sooner put the word *fun* with *flu shot*. Or *onion pancake*. Or *Scutigera coleoptrata*.

It was hard to say what the worst part of group projects was. Sometimes it was the fact that none of the other kids had any ideas and I had to do all the work but share the credit with people who did nothing. Other times the problem was that *everyone* had ideas and no one would listen to mine. Especially not Jenna.

I'd tried explaining this to Mom once, the day I found out I was accepted to Hampshire. That was probably a mistake.

"Why don't you like working with Jenna?" she asked.

But then she interrupted me before I could even start.

"Oh, wait . . . please don't tell me this is about the Betsy Ross Incident," she said. "Just because Jenna got a better grade than you on something back in November?"

I sighed.

"Mom, do you remember what *actually* happened in November?"

Now it was Mom's turn to sigh. "Not really, honey. Can you remind me?"

I took an even deeper breath.

"In November, I had to do a group project on Colonial America with Jenna and Elijah. I was the writer and the director. And I did *all* the research."

"Weren't they supposed to help you with that?" Mom asked.

"Yes, they were," I answered. "But they were *so* slow with the research. And they were using all the wrong websites for sources. Finally I just told them I would do all of it. It was easier that way."

Mom pursed her lips and nodded, waiting for me to continue.

"I told them exactly what they had to do for every part of the skit. And I told Jenna to make sure she spoke extra clearly when she said the best line I wrote."

"And what was that?" Mom asked.

"Well, Jenna was Betsy Ross and Elijah was George Washington," I explained. "After Elijah said, 'What should go on the blue part of the flag?' Jenna was supposed to stand up, point her sewing needle at him, and say, 'They should be stars. Just like YOU, Mr. President!'"

Mom nodded again. "So that isn't what she did?" she asked.

"*No*, that's not what she did at all. She destroyed the skit. Ruined the whole thing. Because after Elijah said, 'What should go on the blue part of the flag?' instead of saying her line like she was supposed to, Jenna looked at the crowd, smiled, then pointed her needle at Elijah and said, 'I'll tell you when I'm done! Stop needling me, will ya!'"

I saw a glimmer in Mom's eyes. "Don't you *dare* laugh," I said. "Everyone else laughed that day, but *you* can't." And they had. The rest of the kids in the class had laughed. The kids from the other visiting fourth-grade classes had laughed. Ms. Puckett and Principal Kleinhoffer had positively cracked up. I had felt dizzy and sick.

"Okay, okay," Mom said. "So that was it? Jenna changed one line?"

I tried to explain. "She changed my *best* line. It was perfect until she did that. She totally messed it up. And everyone loved it. *And* somehow that got her a better grade than mine."

"I see. Did you find out why her grade was better than yours?"

"Ms. Puckett gave me good marks for research and writing, but Jenna got higher scores than me for creativity and participation. And she barely even participated! She always gets what she wants without even trying."

"I don't think that's true," Mom said. "Things aren't always so smooth for Jenna."

"I disagree. Things are actually always very smooth for Jenna. Everyone thinks she's funny. Everyone thinks she's cute, so she gets away with everything. And when she *does* get in a little bit of trouble, she doesn't care. Nothing bothers her."

"I think you'd be surprised," Mom said. "Jenna doesn't always have an easy time in school. Uncle Rex told me she was so proud of the grade she got on that project."

"Well, it was totally unfair," I said. "And it definitely helped convince me I should be at a different school."

Mom reached out and smoothed my hair behind my ears. "Elf, I'm excited for you, for the opportunities you'll have at Hampshire. That's why Dad and I agreed to let you switch to a school like that, with smaller classes and more resources. We know you'll get to do things there that you didn't do at Cottonwood. But you should know there will always be things you think are unfair, no matter where you are."

• • •

I didn't tell Mom about the other thing that happened on the day I asked Ms. Puckett about our grades. That when Jenna found out I'd told the teacher about her changing the script, she was mad. Really mad.

"Why did you have to tell Ms. Puckett about the line change?" she asked.

"I wanted her to know it wasn't right," I said. "I worked really hard on that script."

"Everyone knows how hard you work, Elfie," Jenna said. "It's like the *only* thing everyone knows about you. You work hard and get perfect grades. You're famous for it. Why couldn't you let me get a better grade than you, just this once?"

"It didn't seem fair," I explained. "I wanted it to be fair."

"God, Elfie, you're such a tattletale," Jenna had said that day before storming off to the bus. Then she had turned around and added, "No wonder you don't have any friends."

Of course that hurt a little. Because I was just trying to stand up for myself. And because Jenna was my cousin. But mostly it hurt because she was right.

CHAPTER 6

I tried to shake off the Betsy Ross memory and think positively. After all, this was Hampshire Academy, a place of Honor and Excellence. Certainly group projects would be different here, and no one would say my ideas were boring. No one would take credit for my work. No one would add jokes to my scripts at the last minute. I decided to keep an open mind and wait for the Honor and Excellence to work their magic.

"You've done a lot of sitting this morning," Teacher Olivia said, "so before we start the group project, why don't you take a minute to stretch and get some water if you need to. When we come back to our seats, I think it would be a good idea to do quick introductions with the other students at your table. I'd like you to give them two pieces of information: your name and your favorite thing about Hampshire Academy. Elfie and Sierra, since you're our brand-new

Eyasses, you can instead talk about why you wanted to come to Hampshire Academy."

As I waited in line for the water fountain (clean and shiny, with a special bottle-filling attachment), I thought about how I'd answer that second question. Why did I want to go to Hampshire Academy? I wasn't sure where to begin. There were so many reasons. I'd first started thinking about it when my math coach, Mr. Abrams, told my parents he thought I would "thrive" at a school like Hampshire, with "unlimited resources" and a "brilliant" math and science program. When Mom and Dad said they thought I was thriving just fine at Cottonwood—and for a lot less money, since it was a public school—Mr. Abrams told them that Hampshire gave financial aid to students who demonstrated need. I could tell Dad started thinking about it then, but Mom still wasn't convinced. Then she poked around online and saw that the average class size at Hampshire was just twelve kids. And that the cafeteria served organic apples. (Organic apples are a big thing for Mom. She always says she'd buy all organic food if we could afford it, but it's expensive, so she has to pick and choose. But she read somewhere that it's especially important to get organic apples, because pesticides can soak through their thin skin. So that's what we get. Some parents splurge on expensive shoes or devices . . . my mom buys organic apples.) Anyway, she began taking the idea more seriously.

That's how Mom and Dad started thinking about Hampshire. I was hooked as soon as Mr. Abrams mentioned it. Even though Mom and Dad said I was "thriving" at Cottonwood, I wasn't so sure. I mean, I always got good grades (perfect grades, really), but wouldn't real "thriving" include more than that?

So when *Olivia* (so weird to think of a teacher by her first name) asked us to return to our seats and share our reasons for going to Hampshire with our tablemates, I didn't know what to say. I'd just met Colton and Sierra. How could I tell them that I hoped I'd fit in here? That I'd been told I could "thrive"? That my mom was excited about the organic apples?

Luckily, I didn't have to go first. Colton started right away, in a bored voice that made it sound like he'd answered this question a hundred times already.

"I guess my favorite thing about Hampshire is the fields. We have way better soccer and lacrosse fields than Robbins Country Day School. They don't even have concession stands there!"

I didn't have any response to that. Cottonwood didn't have "fields"; it just had a playground. And definitely no concession stands. Sierra seemed to be at a similar loss for words.

Colton sighed, like he couldn't believe he was stuck at a table with two Eyasses who didn't care about lacrosse fields and concession stands.

"Okay, one of you guys go," he said in a bored voice. "You're supposed to say why you came here."

"Oh, okay," I said. "Well, it's just a really good school."

"Right," Colton said. "Obviously."

But Sierra nodded. "Same reason for me," she said. I felt an urge to high-five her. "Plus, I love science, and they have a great science program; look at all that cool equipment."

That was a good answer. I'd been eyeing the science equipment ever since walking into the classroom; why hadn't I thought to say that? Sierra seemed like someone I could be friends with—real, actual friends.

I started planning how that could go. Since she liked science too, Sierra could come to my house and I'd show her my collection of rocks and minerals. We could even have a sleepover and use my telescope. And I wouldn't have to worry about her touching my things because she seemed to understand how valuable scientific equipment is.

I imagined we'd have so much fun that Sierra would also invite me to sleep over at *her* house. I wondered what her house was like. Maybe she had an even better rock and mineral collection than I did. Hold on . . . maybe she had an earthworm habitat! (An earthworm habitat is something I've always wanted, but Mom and Dad always say no. They claim that if I'm afraid of the cave crickets in our laundry room, I shouldn't have pet earthworms, ignoring my explanation that crawly insects are a completely different thing from slithery invertebrates. I'd be a great earthworm habitat owner. At least I think I would. Probably.)

"What about you?" Sierra asked Colton. "Why did you come to school here?"

"I'm not supposed to answer that question," Colton said. "I'm not new."

"Yeah, but I'm just curious," Sierra said. "Besides, I think we have time." She gestured toward Teacher Olivia, who seemed to be deep in conversation with a group at the front of the room.

Colton sighed again. "I've always known I'd go to Hampshire Academy. My dad went here. So did my grandfather and my uncle. My sister still goes here; she's in the upper school." (The "upper school" is what Hampshire calls high school. I guess that explained how Colton and the teacher knew each other; maybe she had also taught his sister.)

I had another question. "But how did you know for sure that you'd get in?" Hampshire Academy has a very selective admissions policy. I had to write an essay, get recommendation letters from my teachers at Cottonwood, meet an admissions officer for an interview, and take a test. I didn't know I'd get in until the day I got my acceptance letter. And then we had to wait to see if I'd get the scholarship I needed, since Mom and Dad couldn't pay for it on their own.

But Colton laughed at my question. "I just knew, okay? Do you guys know what the library here is called?"

"The Palmer Library," Sierra said.

"Right," Colton said. "Did you happen to catch my last name?"

I glanced at the falcon with his name on the table again. "Palmer."

"Right again." Colton nodded. "That library is state-of-the-art, and it pretty much wouldn't exist without big donations from my grandfather. There's no way I wasn't getting in."

I didn't realize that, that you could automatically go to a private school just because someone in your family donated money to it. It didn't seem fair.

• • •

But I wouldn't get to find out how state-of-the-art the library was, or how amazing the science equipment was, or if Sierra was going to be my first real school friend, since it turned out that I only had a few hours left as a Hampshire Falcon. I would never even make it past being an Eyass.

CHAPTER 7

After we finished our awkward introductions, Teacher Olivia said it was time for a team-building science challenge. I wasn't fooled; I knew that was just another way of saying "group project." Still, I tried to be optimistic. I wasn't so sure how helpful Colton would be, but Sierra was a promising partner.

Olivia gave each table two bags of marshmallows and a box of toothpicks. She walked back to the front of the class, looked at us, and said, "These are your directions: Build the tallest structure you can. Use just your brains and your hands. No other tools."

A boy at the front of the room raised his hand. "What kind of structure?" he asked.

"I have given you all the instructions you need," Olivia said. "A tall structure. No tools. If you need more supplies, ask me; we have plenty. The rest is up to you."

This was already different from doing projects at Cottonwood. Ms. Puckett would probably have given us tons of instructions first, answered about fifty questions, and repeatedly told everyone not to eat the marshmallows. (That was another thing: we definitely wouldn't have had unlimited supplies at Cottonwood; anyone who had a marshmallow craving or broke a toothpick would have been out of luck.)

It was a little unsettling, jumping into a project with basically no directions. Especially since the ability to follow precise directions is one of my strong points. I could tell some of my classmates felt the same way, because I saw them looking around the room with confused faces, hoping to see what other groups were doing to get started.

I was tempted to do the same thing, but I resisted the urge. I didn't want to be accused of cheating and breaking the honor code.

So I focused on my own table, where Colton had already ripped open the bags and strewn marshmallows all over the table. Sierra was carefully removing toothpicks from the box and setting them down.

"Okay, this is super easy," Colton said. "You just have to make sure you scale it right. The height-to-base ratio should be five to seven."

"What do you mean?" Sierra asked.

"It's basic architecture," Colton answered. "It should be

seven marshmallows wide at the base, and five marshmallows high. But since we want to make it tall, we'd do multiples of that. Like fifteen marshmallows high and twenty-one marshmallows wide at the base. Anyone who's ever built a block tower should know this stuff."

Sierra's cheeks turned a little pink.

"Yes, but these aren't blocks," I pointed out. "They're marshmallows and toothpicks. They have different properties that we need to keep in mind."

Colton frowned at me. I had a feeling he wasn't used to being challenged.

"Okay, what *properties* are you worried about?" he asked me.

"I'm not *worried*," I said. "I just think we might have to experiment because we've never built with these before. And they're soft, smooshy, and a little sticky. Those are three properties that blocks don't have."

"I'm not sure *smooshy* counts as a property," he said. "In fact, I don't think that's even a word."

I think seeing me standing up to Colton must have made Sierra feel brave, because she chimed in.

"Yeah, let's just experiment with them," she said. "I don't know how we'd measure ratios anyway, without any tools."

Colton let out a sigh of disgust. "You don't have to measure anything. You just count. Seven marshmallows are seven marshmallows wide. Five marshmallows are five marshmallows high."

"But that assumes they're all uniform in size," I said. "And that the toothpicks are stuck into them the same amount."

"Of course they're uniform," he said, narrowing his eyes at me. "They're made in a *factory*. Here, I'll measure them and show you." He reached into his backpack and took out his phone.

"Whoa, what are you doing?" I asked.

"This has a measuring app on it," he said, pressing his home button. "It'll prove all the marshmallows are the same."

"That's a tool," I said. "We aren't supposed to use anything other than marshmallows and toothpicks."

"Yeah, she's right," Sierra agreed. "I don't think that's allowed."

I looked toward the front of the room to see what Olivia was doing. She didn't seem to be paying much attention to the class; in fact, she was typing on her computer. I wanted her to look over and see Colton with his phone.

"You guys are ridiculous." Colton rolled his eyes. "It's not like this is some serious exam. It's just a stupid first-day game."

"But all the headmaster talked about this morning was the honor code," I said. "We're not going to break it on day one."

Colton laughed. "You think the rest of these kids give a rip about the honor code? This place is so cutthroat, all they care about is making the tallest tower, and I'm sure they'll find ways around the directions. I don't even know why I'm listening to you guys."

Maybe group projects here wouldn't be so great after all.

Colton turned his phone on again and started typing something into it.

"What are you doing?" I asked.

"Searching marshmallow towers online," he answered. "So I can show you how it should really be done."

"Are you kidding me?" I said. "That's flat-out cheating."

"Yeah." Sierra nodded. "You should put that away."

Colton ignored us and kept scrolling down his phone screen. I looked up and saw that Olivia was stepping away from her computer. She was starting to walk to the tables at the front of the room to check on everyone's tower progress. All we had was a table full of marshmallows, a pile of toothpicks, and Colton using his phone.

This was terrible. This was blatant cheating on our first day of school. Even though the building was air-conditioned, I could feel sweat running down the back of my new uniform shirt. I had to do something. But what? I couldn't tell on him or I would get a reputation as a tattletale and ruin any chance I had to make friends here. On the other hand, if we got caught cheating, couldn't we be kicked out?

In my panicked state, there really seemed to be just one solution. I quickly grabbed the phone out of Colton's hand and dropped it into my backpack.

CHAPTER 8

Colton's jaw dropped, and my face suddenly felt very warm. But I didn't have time to think about what I'd done, because just as the phone disappeared from sight, Olivia arrived at our table.

"How's it going here?" she asked. "Still getting to know each other?"

Sierra looked at me, wide-eyed. She had seen me take the phone.

"Yes, everything's fine," Colton said. "We're still talking about how much we love Hampshire, but we're going to get started very soon."

Olivia smiled. "Glad to hear it."

I took two marshmallows with shaky hands, not daring to make eye contact with Colton. I waited to see if he'd reach into my backpack for his phone.

But he didn't have a chance. At that moment, the head-master's voice came over the PA system.

"Good morning again, Falcons and Eyasses! By this point I trust you all know what that term means," he said with a chuckle. "I hope your morning sessions are going well, but now it's time to interrupt them for a time-honored Hampshire tradition. Please gather your things and meet me on the front steps of Palmer Library in five minutes!"

"Okay, group, let's head out," Olivia said. "You might not be returning to this room soon, so bring your backpacks. I'll save your marshmallow structures for tomorrow." She seemed a little annoyed about the group project being inter-rupted, but I guess nothing could get in the way of "a time-honored Hampshire tradition."

Everyone started picking up their backpacks and shuf-fling toward the door. I expected Colton to demand his phone back, but he didn't say a word. He was moving faster than anyone else, like he couldn't wait to get out of the class-room.

"Hey, sorry about your phone," I said, chasing after him. "I panicked a little. Here, I'll give it back." I dug around in my backpack. I'd been so frazzled that I wasn't sure which pocket I'd dropped it into.

Colton rolled his eyes. "Forget it, Marshmallow Po-lice," he said. "I'll find a way to get you back later." Then he sprinted out of the room. I was confused. Had he meant to say "I'll find a way to get *it* back later"? Meaning his phone? Or did he really think he had to get *me* back for something? I began to feel nervous.

I followed him, but he was lost in the crowd of kids in front of me in the hallway. Zach and the other welcome leaders were waving little Hampshire Academy flags and yelling, "This way, this way; everyone come with us!"

I zipped my backpack and hoisted it onto my shoulder. I figured I'd see Colton when we all arrived at our destination, whatever that was.

We followed the welcome leaders and their little flags out of the building and across a courtyard to Palmer Library. On the steps of the library were the headmaster, some other staff members I didn't recognize, and two giant falcons (one was a real falcon in a giant birdcage, the other was someone dressed as the Falcon mascot). Beside the Falcon mascot was a woman holding a megaphone.

"HEY, HEY, HEY, FALCONS AND EYASSES!" she yelled into it. "I'm Mara Rosen, and I graduated from Hampshire Academy ten years ago. Now I am honored to be not only your volleyball and field hockey coach, but also the official coordinator of school spirit! Let me hear your spirit, Hampshire; give me a cheer!"

I knew exactly what would happen next. I have never,

ever been in a situation where someone asks for a crowd response and is satisfied with the crowd's first effort. So I knew that all of us would yell half-heartedly and that Mara would say something like "I can't hear you!" or "That's not good enough!" and that we would all yell louder the second time, mostly to get her to stop bugging us about cheering.

And I was right; that is what happened. But I couldn't focus on the cheering or the things Mara was yelling about what a privilege it was to be a Falcon because I was too busy looking for Colton. I didn't see him anywhere. I needed to give him back his phone; I really didn't feel right about still having something that wasn't mine. It was like I had a ticking time bomb in my backpack.

As Mara blew into a harmonica and started singing the opening bars of the school song, I spotted him. He was near the base of the library steps, talking to Headmaster Mulligan. The headmaster was nodding seriously as Colton spoke. He patted Colton on the shoulder, climbed the steps, and stood beside Mara.

When Mara finished singing, Headmaster Mulligan leaned over and whispered something in her ear. She nodded too, then spoke into her megaphone. "Sorry, everyone, but we have a quick interruption. We have a missing item that we need to locate. Can everyone please be silent for a moment?"

As the crowd quieted down, I briefly wondered what was

missing. What could be lost that required all of us to be silent? And what did it have to do with Colton?

Oh. Of course. Just as Headmaster Mulligan pulled out his own phone and started tapping at the screen, I knew what he must be doing. I tried to think fast. . . . What should I do? Announce "I know where it is"? Fish the phone out of my backpack, hold it up in the air, and yell, "I found it"? Create some kind of diversion, like running up and opening the falcon's cage? But before I could decide, a sound started coming out of my backpack. A very loud sound. The very loud sound of someone burping. Because of course that was Colton's ringtone. *Of course* it was.

The group of Falcons and Eyasses who had been cheering on command just moments before had also gotten completely silent on command, so naturally hundreds of heads turned toward the only source of sound in the crowd: me and my belching backpack.

Headmaster Mulligan pointed at me. "You there. Please come forward."

The crowd parted to make a path for me to move toward the front. As I walked, I rummaged around in my backpack, trying to find the phone buried under my notebook, pencil case, tissue packet, and seaweed crisps. With my bag unzipped and hanging open, the burping sound only became louder. A few Falcons in the crowd giggled.

Finally, as I reached the library steps, my fingers located

the phone at the bottom of the backpack. I pulled it out, its belching sounds now unmuffled and louder than ever.

"I found it!" I said in a weak voice, but Headmaster Mulligan did not seem impressed or relieved. Instead, he simply held out his hand for the phone, giving me a look of extreme dismay.

As I placed the phone in the headmaster's hand and looked down to zip up my bag, the burping finally stopped.

Headmaster Mulligan handed the phone to Colton and turned to Mara Rosen, who, like the rest of the student body, was gaping at us to see how this scene would unfold. "Please, carry on," he said, nodding at Mara and gesturing toward her megaphone.

Mara started up a new cheer, and the headmaster beckoned toward Teacher Olivia, who was standing on the edge of the crowd of students. "Will you three please join me inside?" he asked, looking at her, Colton, and me.

As I followed them back to the building we'd come from, my body felt a way it had never felt before. It was like it didn't know whether to faint, throw up, or cry. Or maybe all three. My face felt like it was full of pine needles. Somehow my legs managed to move the rest of me slowly back to the large front doors of the building.

Headmaster Mulligan held the door open for me and gestured inside. "After you, Miss Oster. Let's go to my office, shall we?"

I had a fleeting thought about what a weird place this was, where teachers were called by their first names, but the headmaster called me Miss Oster.

I followed Olivia and Colton into the office. Headmaster Mulligan joined us and closed the door behind him.

"This is a very serious matter, Miss Oster," he said. "Mr. Palmer reported that his phone was missing, and now it appears that you took it."

My voice faltered. "I . . . There was confusion about our project, and—"

Headmaster Mulligan interrupted me. "Miss Oster, I'm not sure how carefully you paid attention to my opening statements this morning. But it seems that you have missed something crucial. The Hampshire Academy honor code is our most important tradition. If we do not adhere to it, we betray everything we value."

Nausea quickly became the main feeling in my body. "Well, yes, but I only took the phone because . . ." Because why? Because Colton was about to cheat? Jenna had said it wasn't surprising that I didn't have any friends when she found out I'd told Ms. Puckett about how she changed our Betsy Ross skit. Was I going to tell on Colton for this? That wasn't how I wanted to start life at my new school. This was supposed to be the place where I'd do well and be happy and make friends. And *thrive*.

I glanced at Colton. The smirk he'd had on his face this

morning was nothing compared to the smug grin he was wearing now.

Headmaster Mulligan continued. "Part of the honor code includes a zero-tolerance policy for behaviors such as theft. I'm afraid that in light of this discovery, we have to consider whether you can continue as a student here. We will call your parents to discuss this; you can stay in the waiting room until they arrive."

Was this really happening? I looked from Headmaster Mulligan, who appeared quite serious, to Olivia, who seemed more shocked. Her face was flushed, and she was holding her hand over her mouth. "Do you have anything to add here, Colton?" she asked.

Colton actually looked even redder than Olivia did. He made a strange sound, kind of like a cross between a hiccup and a cough. "Um, no, I guess not," he said once he found his voice.

Headmaster Mulligan gave him a long look. "She took your phone, yes?" he asked.

"Um, well . . . yeah," Colton said.

"Very well, then," said Headmaster Mulligan. "I'll make the call."

My body knew what to do then. A giant tear slid down my face onto the perfect, spotless, shiny wooden floor of Hampshire Academy.

CHAPTER 9

Headmaster Mulligan was in his office with the door closed when Mom came to pick me up. She looked stunned.

"Elfie, I'm stunned," she said. "What's this about you breaking the honor code? What happened?"

"I can't tell you right now," I said.

Mom looked around. No one else was in the waiting room with us; Headmaster Mulligan's assistant had stepped away from her desk.

"I think you'd *better* tell me," she said. "This is serious, Elfie."

"I mean I don't think I physically *can* tell you," I said. "Not without crying."

Mom sat beside me. "Elf, please try."

"They think I stole something," I said. "Someone's

phone." I choked out the last words; it was too horrible to admit to Mom.

"What in the world?" Mom said. "That's not you! Why would they say that?"

I could only shake my head; I was crying too hard to explain. Mom put her arm around my shoulders and squeezed me close to her; it felt good, but it also made me cry even harder.

The heavy wooden office door opened with a creak, and Headmaster Mulligan motioned for Mom and me to come in. He sat in a big leather chair behind his desk, and Mom and I sat in two smaller chairs facing it. For a few long seconds, the only sound in the room was my sniffling. I am not someone who cries often, but once I start, I find it extremely difficult to stop. Especially when I'm crying very hard because, for example, my life has just been ruined.

Mom started rubbing my back, and Headmaster Mulligan handed me a box of tissues. I got the feeling this was not the first time someone had cried in his office.

Since I was still having a hard time speaking, Mom took the lead. "Can you tell me what is going on?" she asked the headmaster. "Elfie says she's been accused of stealing someone's phone?"

"Yes." Headmaster Mulligan nodded. "Another student reported that his phone was missing, so we called it to listen for the ring, and it was discovered in Elfie's backpack."

"There must have been some kind of mistake," Mom said. "Elfie is not a thief. Maybe this boy put his phone in Elfie's backpack by accident."

Headmaster Mulligan pressed his fingertips together and looked at Mom pityingly. "Elfie admits that she took the phone," he said quietly.

Mom turned to me, speechless except for one word. "Elfie?"

What could I say? How could I possibly explain that I knew I had made a mistake, but that I did it to keep Colton from making an even bigger one? Would it even matter, the word of an Eyass against the word of a Falcon whose grandfather donated the school library? And if they did believe me, and Colton got in trouble, would I be guaranteeing that I wouldn't have any friends at this school either?

I searched my brain for a way to explain what happened without getting Colton into trouble. And without getting myself into even deeper trouble.

"I . . . I guess I misunderstood something Colton said. I thought he was going to use his phone to help with a project we were working on, and we weren't supposed to do that."

"So you took it and put it in your backpack?" Headmaster Mulligan didn't have to say what he was thinking, which was that he considered my choice a very poor one.

"I don't know why I did that," I said, which was the truth.

"It's up to the teachers to enforce the rules, Ms. Oster,"

the headmaster said. "If Olivia thought Colton was doing something wrong, she could have determined the consequences. It's her classroom."

For the first time, a flicker of doubt crossed Mom's face. She knew rules were important to me, and that sometimes I tried to enforce them myself.

"Do you think we could call Olivia in to meet with us?" Mom asked. "And maybe this boy . . . Colton? Is that his name?"

Headmaster Mulligan sighed. "As you might imagine, the first day of school is very busy for students and teachers alike. And also for me."

"After school, then?" Mom said.

"Olivia and I will both be in a staff meeting this afternoon. But there is a process—"

Mom interrupted him. "Are you honestly going to make a decision as serious as expelling a student this quickly?"

"As I was saying," Headmaster Mulligan continued, "there is a process here by which such decisions are made. We have an honor code review board that meets as needed to review honor code infractions and determine consequences."

"When will that happen?"

"I will have to confer with the review board members and find out what their availability is. This is a bit of an unusual case; we have never had an honor code concern this early in the school year."

Mom sat back in her chair a little. "So Elfie can stay at Hampshire? At least until the review board makes its decision?"

Headmaster Mulligan shook his head. "I'm afraid not. Our policy is that students who are suspected of honor code infractions are suspended until the board's decision is made."

"Suspended?" I had never heard Mom's voice go so high.

"Yes, but only until the board reaches a decision." He saw the desperate look on Mom's face and added, "I will tell them that we would like a timely response."

Before Mom could protest further, Headmaster Mulligan's assistant knocked on the door.

"Yes, come in," the headmaster called.

"Pardon the interruption, Headmaster, but you're needed in the planetarium to introduce the new astrophysics teacher. The class is starting soon."

"Oh yes, I'd completely forgotten." Headmaster Mulligan stood quickly from his desk. "I'm sorry to cut this short. We'll be sure to let you know as soon as the review board schedules its meeting."

Mom threw her arms into the air as he scurried out of the room. "Okay, well, I guess that's it," she said, huffing in disbelief as she stood and picked up her purse. "Let's go; get your backpack."

"Wait. What do you mean, 'that's it'?"

"You heard the headmaster. It sounds like our hands are

tied until these *honor review* people decide when they're going to meet. I mean, Dad and I will do what we can to rush it along, but I'm not sure how much power we have here."

"So what do I do for school until then?"

Mom sighed. "Well, off the top of my head, it seems that the obvious answer is—"

"No. No! Do not say it, Mom. Don't say it. Don't say it. Do *not* say—"

"The first day of school at Cottonwood is in two weeks."

CHAPTER 10

I couldn't bear to talk to Mom during the ride home. As soon as she got in the car and said "Elfie . . . ," I stopped her.

"Can we please just be quiet for now?" Today had been bad enough; I had no strength to listen to Mom tell me why going back to Cottonwood was a good idea. Luckily, Mom nodded and buckled her seat belt.

I was hoping to run upstairs to my room as soon as I walked through the door, but Dad was waiting in the kitchen when we got back, wanting to know what happened. I somehow managed to squeak out my side of the story about Colton and the phone.

"That doesn't sound like stealing to me," Dad said. "Did you explain all this to the headmaster?"

"He didn't give us much of a chance," Mom said. She told Dad about having to wait for the honor review board's decision.

I shrugged. "I'm not sure how much my side of the story will even matter. Colton's grandpa bought the library; they're not going to take my word over his."

"What do you mean, he 'bought the library'?" Dad asked.

"His grandfather gave the school so much money that they named the library after him," I explained. "It's called the Palmer Library, and that's his last name."

Mom's face got red, the way it does when she hears something upsetting on the news. "That shouldn't matter," she said.

I shrugged. "Okay," I said, "but I didn't want to start life at a new school by telling on someone. It was bad enough that I grabbed his phone. This was supposed to be the place where I finally made friends."

Now Mom looked like *she* wanted to cry. "I know, honey," she said quietly. "But this boy doesn't sound like the kind of friend you'd want to have."

"We're going to see if we can fight this, Elf," Dad said. "Is there anyone else who knows your side of the story?"

"Sierra," I said. "She was the other kid at our table. She saw me take the phone. But then we left the room, and I never saw her again after that." Sierra had seemed like someone I could be friends with; maybe she would stick up for me? But could I ask her to tell on Colton too? Not that it really mattered; *her* grandfather hadn't bought the library either.

"Okay," Mom said. "We're going to make some calls tomorrow. For now, why don't you just relax. Are you hungry?"

"*No*, I'm not hungry. And how can I possibly relax after the worst day of my life? Especially when you said I have to go back to Cottonwood?"

"She does?" Dad asked.

"I didn't say she *has* to do anything," Mom said. "It was just a thought. We have to wait and see if we'll have an answer from Hampshire in time."

"Okay." Dad nodded. "So don't worry just yet, Elf. You might not have to go back to Cottonwood after all."

CHAPTER 11

I had to go back to Cottonwood.

Mom and Dad got an email from Headmaster Mulligan the next afternoon saying that "because of other commitments, the volunteers who serve on the honor review board will not be able to meet until October."

"October?" I said when they told me. "That's over a month from now!"

Dad sighed. "I know, Elf. It stinks. But we're somewhat powerless here."

I threw my hands up. "Okay. Well, I guess that settles it. I'll just have to homeschool until then." I thought maybe if I pretended we'd never discussed the possibility of my returning to Cottonwood, Mom and Dad wouldn't remember.

It didn't work.

"Who exactly would be homeschooling you?" Mom asked. "Dad and I both have to go to work. Rhoda has her nursing school classes during the day." Mom and Dad had both taken off to stay home with me today because I was so upset about yesterday. But I knew that couldn't happen every day.

"I can homeschool myself!" I said. "I'd be very good at it!"

"Well, true as that might be," Dad said, "it's also illegal. We can't leave a ten-year-old home alone, in charge of her own education."

"And since Cottonwood's start date is two weeks later than Hampshire's," Mom said, "you could start on the first day of school there too."

"Lucky me," I grumbled. "I get to have *two* terrible first days of school."

"Who says the one at Cottonwood has to be terrible?" Dad said, putting on a chipper voice.

"*I* say so, all right? Don't waste your time trying to convince me otherwise." Mom closed her eyes and gave Dad a little head shake, which I knew meant "Don't try to give her a pep talk now."

I turned on my heel and ran upstairs.

In my room, I crawled under my covers and thought about how my life was ruined. How was I going to go back to Cottonwood Elementary and tell everyone I'd been kicked out of Hampshire Academy on my very first day? What would Ms. Puckett think? And Principal Kleinhoffer? And Jenna. *Ugh*, I'd have to tell Jenna.

All the terrible thoughts got to be too much for my brain to hold. Everything that had happened yesterday had been hard enough, but hearing that I'd definitely have to go back to Cottonwood was the last straw. My nose started running and tears began streaming down my cheeks. I put my pillow over my face so no one would hear me crying; I didn't want my parents to come check on me.

A while later, I heard the click of my bedroom doorknob as Mom peeked in. I still didn't want to talk. I pretended to be asleep. But the funny thing about pretending to be asleep is that it can make you fall asleep for real, and I'm pretty sure I conked out as soon as Mom tiptoed down the hall. It was still hours from bedtime, but my body couldn't take any more of feeling this lousy.

CHAPTER 12

Even though I fell asleep early, I could have stayed in bed the whole next day. When Mom came in to say good morning, I tried faking sleep. She sat on my bed and gave my leg a little shake. I kept pretending. She cooed "Elllfieee" in her soft morning voice. I still pretended. Mom started talking anyway.

"Okay, I know you're awake," she said. "I just heard your alarm going off. Also, I can tell by the way you're breathing."

Was that true? I tried to slow my breathing down to seem more asleep. But Mom kept talking.

"I'm staying home again today. I know you're having a hard time," she said. "And I understand you wanting to hide from the world, but you're going to have to surface at some point." She patted my leg and stood up. "I can make cinnamon toast, if you're hungry."

I wasn't hungry. And I didn't want to "surface" to talk to Mom or anyone else. I was perfectly content to wallow in the depths of my covers.

Eventually Mom put two pieces of toast and some milk on my bedside table. After she left, I stopped fake-sleeping and ate. Mom must have been lurking in the hall, because as soon as I slid the plate closer, she popped her head into my doorway and said, "One more thing. Uncle Rex just found out he got a gig tonight, and Aunt Steph is traveling again. Jenna's coming here for dinner."

I have always liked the way there is a word for almost everything. For example, the little groove between your nose and your top lip is called your *philtrum*. A *harrier* is a cross-country runner. If you are *supine,* it means you're lying down on your back (*recumbent* means the same thing). There is even a word that means "cannot be described by words." That word is *ineffable*. And you could say I had *ineffable* feelings of doom about the news that Jenna was coming over for dinner. *Annoyance* was not a strong enough word. Neither was *irritation*. Even *dread* didn't describe it. It was *ineffable*, the way I felt about seeing Jenna right after I got kicked out of Hampshire.

I know that sounds dramatic. She's just my cousin; what's the big deal? But our whole lives, I have been good at one thing: school. Jenna has been good at everything else: sports, making friends, making people laugh, choosing outfits, braiding hair. Now Jenna would know I had failed at the only thing I was ever good at.

When I would complain about Jenna to Dad, he'd say, "I know you guys are different, but she's a good kid too." Mom would say, "She is family, and you have to find a way to get along." The only person who seemed to understand was Rhoda. If I told her that Jenna didn't pay attention to me, or rolled her eyes when I complained about a test being too easy, or changed the best line in my Betsy Ross script, she would nod along and say something like "*Urft.* Jenna just doesn't get you, does she?" (Rhoda likes using funny-sounding words like *goober* and *kerfuffle. Urft* is a word she made up, and it's the one she uses most often. It means "That's frustrating" or "How annoying" or "I understand why you're out of sorts.") And then she'd suggest we do something fun, like watch *Superstars of Science* or make chocolate turtle brownies.

Rhoda was right. Jenna didn't get me. *Rhoda* got me. Always.

And then I realized there was one person I felt like talking to.

I got out of bed and walked into the kitchen. Mom was drinking tea and working at her computer. "Are you sure you don't want to go to work today?" I asked her.

"I'm sure," Mom said. "I feel like I'm more needed here right now. Keisha understands." Keisha was Mom's boss at the law firm where she worked. "Besides, I can check emails from home if I have to."

"Oh," I said. "Okay."

Mom faked a hurt look. "Why? Are you trying to get rid of me?"

Sort of? I thought. But I didn't say that.

"No," I said. "I was just wondering." I tried to think of how to say that I really wanted to see Rhoda. It's not that Mom or Dad got jealous, exactly, when there were times that I wanted to talk to Rhoda instead of them. Mom would even say, "I'm glad you feel like you can confide in her so much." But I knew that when really big things like this came up, they wanted to be my chief problem solvers.

"I was also wondering . . . ," I said, "did you tell Rhoda about what happened at Hampshire?"

Mom took her hand off her computer mouse and turned to look at me. "I did, hon; I hope that's okay. I thought you might appreciate not having to tell her yourself. Also, I had to explain why we didn't need her to come."

"Yes, that's fine. What did she say?" I asked.

"She said she felt like she'd been kicked in the stomach, and I said that's how we all felt too. She also said to tell you *she* knows what a good kid you are, and that she loves you."

I nodded. I thought I'd cried all the tears I had yesterday, but I started to feel more coming to the surface.

Mom reached out and rubbed my arm. "Rhoda will come back tomorrow, okay?" I nodded again.

I thought about asking if I could call Rhoda, but what if she didn't answer? Then Mom might try to get me to talk to her instead, and I was really in more of a talk-to-Rhoda mood than a talk-to-Mom mood.

There was only one thing to do. Go to the Important Jar. The Important Jar was something Rhoda started when I was about four years old. Mom and Dad had taken me to the zoo for the first time, and I couldn't wait to tell Rhoda all about the different animals I saw. But when she arrived at our house the next morning, I couldn't remember the names of all of them, and I got so mad. "You weren't here when we got home!" I yelled at her. "And now I forget some of the important things I wanted to tell you!"

Rhoda went onto the zoo's website and clicked through the pictures to help me remember the animals I'd seen. But then she said, "I have an idea. Since I'm not here all the time, why don't we find a way to help you remember things you want to tell me when I'm at my house and you're here."

She found an empty pickle jar under the kitchen sink and made a label for it that said "The Important Jar." I drew pictures of some of the zoo animals I'd seen and taped them to the jar too.

Rhoda put the jar on my dresser beside a little notepad. "Okay," she'd said. "This is the Important Jar. Anytime I'm not here and you think of something important you want to tell me, write it on a piece of paper and put it in the jar. Then when I come to your house later, you can show me everything you wrote."

I wasn't so sure. "What about spelling?" I'd asked her. I was just learning how to write, and Rhoda knew I got frustrated if I didn't know how to spell a word. (Even when I was four, I was very serious about getting things just right.)

Rhoda nodded. "Well, my advice about spelling is to do the best you can, and I think you'd be surprised at how I'll still be able to read words that aren't spelled just right. Or you could ask your parents to help you. *Or* you could draw a picture."

"Okay," I'd agreed. And that was how the Important Jar got started. Now it's been on my dresser for six years and still has the pictures I drew of a tiger, a giraffe, and a panda taped to it. Anytime during these six years that I thought of something I wanted to tell Rhoda, I'd write it down and put it in the jar. And somewhere along the way, she started using it too; if I was at a piano lesson or meeting with my math coach and she thought of something she wanted to tell me, it would be there waiting in the Important Jar when I got home.

So after I talked to Mom, I went up to my room. I wrote

the following notes on little pieces of paper, folded them up, and put them in the Important Jar:

- I can't believe I messed up so badly.
- Mom and Dad are being nice but I'm afraid they're really disappointed in me.
- I don't want to go back to Cottonwood, or Hampshire, or any other school, ever again.
- What is going to happen to me?

CHAPTER 13

After I put the last piece of paper into the Important Jar, I collapsed onto my bed again. I was not usually a person who took naps. It always seemed like such a waste of time. Mom, Dad, and Rhoda say I didn't even like taking naps when I was a baby. But what else was I going to do? I wasn't going back to Hampshire Academy. I certainly wasn't going shopping for a first-day-of-school outfit for Cottonwood; I couldn't care less what I was going to wear there. Hiding under my covers seemed like the only way to escape from the shambles my life had become.

I must have fallen asleep for a while, because Dad was home when I woke up. He was peering into my room, tapping on the door, and doing the same little voice Mom had done in the morning: "Ellllfiieeee, wake up, sleepy girl."

I opened one eye and looked at him.

"Wow, a nap, huh?" he said. "That's so unlike you. How are you feeling today?"

I shrugged.

"Yeah, I get it," he said. (*Did he? How could he possibly get it?* I wondered.)

"Hey . . . I know what will take your mind off your troubles," Dad said. "Shucking corn! Jenna's coming over soon, and I thought you guys could work on that together."

Nothing like waking up from a nap and being asked to do two of my least favorite things: hang out with Jenna and shuck corn.

"Do I have to?" I asked. I searched my brain for an example of something else I had to do so I could get out of it. I was coming up empty.

"I think it would be good for you," Dad said. "You've spent enough time by yourself up here in your room." He pulled opened my curtains. "Check it out! Sunshine!"

I squinted. "I prefer the dark."

"I know you do, Elf," Dad said. "But I want you to try letting a little light in."

• • •

As I walked into the kitchen, Mom announced that Jenna and Uncle Rex had just pulled into the driveway.

"I thought she was only coming for *dinner*," I said. "Not this early."

"Well, aren't you the hostess with the mostest?" Mom swatted me with a dish towel. "Uncle Rex's gig is in Greenville, about half an hour away. He has to get there early to set up, so I told him he could bring Jenna whenever he needed to."

"Why isn't Aunt Steph ever around?"

Mom was quiet for a second. "You know she's busy with work."

"She's *always* busy with work," I complained. "Seems like way more than ever lately. Are they at least bringing Larry?" Larry, Jenna's dog, was the only bright spot in a visit from her.

"No." Mom sounded relieved. "They're boarding him at a kennel tonight just in case. Uncle Rex knows that leaving the dog here is a big ask."

Hmph. Leaving Jenna here seemed like a much bigger "ask" to me, but no one seemed to care for my opinion on the matter.

Uncle Rex works as a lab technician during the day, but he also plays the saxophone in a band. He says that's his "real" job, and that being a lab technician is just to pay the bills. His band plays a few times a month. Sometimes they play in an outdoor amphitheater or a restaurant where kids are allowed, and then Jenna's allowed to go. I've been to some of those shows too. But other times, like tonight, the band plays in a bar where you have to be twenty-one or over to get in. When that happens, we usually wind up with Jenna. Lucky us.

"Hey, Teeney!" Uncle Rex called as he opened the door. Mom's name is Justine, but Uncle Rex has always called her Teeney. He's the only one who's allowed to do that. It's kind of funny, since Mom is actually pretty tall.

"Hello, Brother," Mom said. "Have you eaten? Dinner's not ready yet, but you can take a turkey sandwich or something for the road."

"It's okay; I'll grab a burger at the bar. Thanks, though."

Uncle Rex reached out and rubbed my hair. "Hey, Elf. Sorry to hear you're having a stinker of a week," he said, as though getting kicked out of Hampshire Academy was something minor, like having a bad cold or losing your house keys.

I couldn't really focus on responding to his comment, though, because my eyes were zooming in on what he was carrying.

"Is that Jenna's sleeping bag and pillow?" I asked. This was not okay. No one had said anything about Jenna sleeping over.

"Wow, nothing gets by you," said a sarcastic voice from the doorway. It was Jenna, just now making her way inside. She had clearly been delayed by something fascinating on her phone screen. She didn't even look up from it as she joined us in the kitchen.

"Your mom said Jenna could sleep over if she needed to.

These gigs in Greenville can run really late," Uncle Rex explained.

This was too much. Why did Jenna have to be *our* responsibility, and all night long?

"Remind me why your mom can't take care of you?" I asked.

"Elfie." Mom said my name in this sharp way she has where the *f* sound becomes like a tiny dagger. I saw her and Uncle Rex exchange a quick look, and Jenna's cheeks were pink as she stared down at her phone.

"I told you Aunt Steph is traveling for work," Mom said. "And we're happy to have you anytime, honey." She gave Jenna an awkward hug that went unreturned because of course Jenna was still holding her phone in both hands.

Anytime we weren't in school, it was like Jenna's phone was surgically attached to her. She only looked up from it when an adult made her put it down.

I didn't have my own phone. Mom and Dad said I couldn't get one until I was thirteen, but I didn't really see the need for one anyway. I used my computer for homework, watching videos, and researching things that interested me (like challenging math problems, world and American history, and the geographic regions different harmful insects might be found in). Jenna used her phone for texting other kids and sending them cute and funny pictures. This was not something I needed to be able to do. And the disaster with Colton was further support for my conviction that kids our age had no business owning their own phones.

Dad came in holding a big paper bag.

"Hey, Rex. Hope the gig goes okay." Dad and Uncle Rex were really different. Dad was a librarian, and he loved books (no surprise there) and going to peaceful places like parks and quiet restaurants. Uncle Rex liked loud music and big parties. He was always grabbing me, mom, or Jenna by the hand to try to get us to dance. (He never had to convince Aunt Steph. She was a born dancer like him.)

But Dad and Uncle Rex still got along really well. Mom always said that the two of them were like circles in a Venn diagram, where most things were different. But the places where the circles overlapped (good food, their senses of humor, and a love of scary movies) held them together.

"I told Elfie these girls have their work cut out for them." Dad tipped the bag forward so we could all see the ears of corn inside.

"Why is there so much?" I asked. "There are only four of us eating."

"We'll send some home with Uncle Rex in case he and Jenna want it later in the week."

Dad handed me the bag. "Take that out to the porch, though. We don't want corn worms inside the house."

I shuddered. My own personal scary movie was about to unfold.

CHAPTER 14

Everyone knows that the scariest part of a horror movie isn't when the monster jumps out of a closet. It's the part right before that, when the main character is slowly reaching toward the closet door. *That's* the part where the audience is screaming, "No, no, don't do it; run away!"

Well, when I shuck corn, every husk is like that closet door for me. Because each time I peel one back, I'm convinced that a sod webworm is going to be on the other side. And if not a sod webworm, then a European corn borer. Or a seed-corn beetle. Maybe a corn leaf aphid. The point is, insects love corn. And that's why you can be sure that in every batch of corn you shuck, there will usually be at least one or two bugs hiding behind a husk, waiting to jump out at you (especially if your parents prefer to buy organic corn, which is grown with minimal pesticide exposure).

I sat on one of the rocking chairs on the porch and put

the bag of corn in front of me, with an empty bag beside it for the husks. Jenna sat in the rocker opposite mine, pulled one knee up to her chest, and started tapping at her phone. Of course.

"Aren't you going to help me?"

"With what?"

"*Shucking the corn,* like my dad asked us to do."

Jenna glanced up from her phone for half a second. "Yeah, in a minute." Then she kept tapping away.

I slowly pulled the husks away from one ear of corn, holding it as far as I could from my face and bracing myself to see a giant insect every time.

Jenna glanced up again. "Why do you do it like that?"

"Like what?"

"So slowly. And so far from your head, like it's going to explode."

She was unbelievable. Not only was she glued to her phone instead of helping me, but she was actually criticizing the way I was doing the job we were *both* supposed to be doing.

I started ripping away at the next ear much more quickly.

"You're so annoying, Jenna. If you're such an expert at shucking corn, why don't you do it yourself and let go of your phone for a ch— AYYYY!"

Jenna had gotten me so worked up that I'd lost all focus. Just as I was about to say "change," I ripped back a stalk to reveal a gigantic slimy monster (more specifically, a European corn borer).

It startled me so much that I flung the ear of corn straight at Jenna's head.

"Hey! What'd you do that for?"

"A corn borer!" I said. "I was surprised. There's a European corn borer on that ear of corn." I scooched back my rocking chair and pointed at the corn borer.

"A *what?*" Jenna said. "This little thing?"

She picked up the ear of corn and, to my great disgust, plucked the corn borer off with her thumb and forefinger and examined it. Because of course—*of course*—Jenna is not only popular and cute and athletic, but she's also not afraid of anything. Including slimy insects.

"Hey, Chubby Squirmy Guy," Jenna said, holding the wriggling wormlike insect up to her face to get a closer look. She was using the same voice other people might use to talk to a puppy.

"What did you call it again?" she asked.

"A European corn borer. That's what it's called."

"You're so weird, Elfie. Why do you have to use the scientific name for everything?"

"As a matter of fact, I don't," I said. "*European corn borer* is its *common* name. *Scientific* names are Latin. If I were going to call it by its scientific name, I would call it *Ostrinia nubilalis.*"

"Ohmigod, you're even weirder than I thought." Jenna

rolled her eyes. "How do you know that? *Why* do you know that?"

"As you may have noticed, I'm not a particularly big fan of insects. Learning as much as I can about them helps them become more familiar to me. Besides, sometimes the common name—like *cave crickets*—is terrifying. So learning the scientific name helps me feel less intimidated."

"Yeah, I can tell that's really working," she muttered, rolling her eyes again. "Well, I'm going to call him Chubby Squirmy Guy."

Jenna set *Ostrinia nubilalis,* aka the European corn borer, aka Chubby Squirmy Guy, on the porch railing. She tore into the next ear of corn, which revealed two corn leaf aphids (scientific name: *Rhopalosiphum maidis;* Jenna names: Tiny Green Guy and Little Green Lady), and a third ear, which was free of insects. She seemed disappointed.

"I have a question," Jenna said as she reached for another ear. "Is that why you wanted to go to that other school? Because they do things like talk about bugs in a different language?"

"Something like that," I said.

She nodded. "What's that place called? Hamster Academy?"

"*Hampshire* Academy," I corrected her, and shook my head. Jenna was a terrible listener.

"Oh. Well, I'm sorry they kicked you out."

"Yes, I'm sure you are," I said. "Now you're stuck with me back at Cottonwood."

"Ugh, Elfie, that's not what I meant. I just know you really wanted to go there, and you're probably upset!" Then she muttered something that sounded like "I don't know why I try."

"What did you say?" I asked.

"Nothing." Jenna looked at the corn in my lap. "Hey, *now* who's not doing their job?" she said, reaching for a fifth ear of corn and noticing that I had barely started my third. "You're just sitting there!"

I hopped up from my chair. "No, I'm not. Now I'm going to the bathroom. Keep up the good work."

I knew that leaving Jenna with the rest of the corn wasn't exactly the right thing to do. But she seemed to genuinely enjoy finding the insects. And I was usually the one doing all the work when we had a chore to do (or a group project). Besides, I wanted to send a clear signal that I was done talking about Hampshire Academy with her. (And I really did have to use the bathroom.)

I went through the dining room on my way back out. Dad was sitting at the table on his laptop, making a serious face as he looked at the screen.

"What's going on?" I asked him.

He looked surprised to see me standing there. "Oh, nothing. Just doing a little research."

But I could see the reflection of the screen in Dad's glasses. It was a familiar purple background with a white falcon logo in the corner. The Hampshire Academy website.

"Why are you on the Hampshire website?" I asked. "What happened?"

"How's that corn coming along?" Dad asked.

"I just came in to use the bathroom. But don't change the subject. Why are you on the Hampshire Academy website?"

Dad sighed. "I was going to wait until Jenna wasn't here to tell you this. But I went online to see what I could learn about the honor code review board at Hampshire."

"Oh." Something in Dad's voice told me I wasn't sure I wanted to hear the rest.

"And, well . . ."

He turned the computer to face me. The heading at the top of the page said "Honor Code Review Board Members," and it was followed by a list of names. At first I wasn't sure why Dad was showing it to me. Then one name near the bottom jumped out at me: Colton R. Palmer IV.

"Colton's on this board?!" I said. "How can that be? He's just a kid!"

"No, it must be his father," Dad said. "Or maybe his grandfather. Did Colton happen to mention what number is after his name?"

I shook my head. "We didn't get to know each other quite that well."

"Right. Well, I'm just thinking . . ."

". . . that I don't have any hope of getting admitted back at Hampshire if someone in Colton's family is on the board that makes those decisions."

Dad turned the computer back to face himself. "I'm not saying that, necessarily. It's just that . . . well, we're all still learning how these things work."

"I already know how these things work," I said. "If you have enough money to buy a library, you can also get anything else you want. Including unfair punishments for other people."

• • •

Jenna had finished shucking the corn by the time I went back out to the porch, something she kept reminding us of throughout dinner. ("This corn is delicious, isn't it? You know, I pretty much shucked it all by myself.")

I didn't even argue with her by pointing out that I had shucked three ears. I didn't have the energy. All I could think about was how there was no way Colton's father, or grandfather, or anyone in his family, would ever let me back into Hampshire Academy.

CHAPTER 15

Jenna didn't sleep over that night. Uncle Rex came by to get her after his show at around midnight. He seemed really tired, but she must have texted him that she wanted to go home. I suspected this because after she fell asleep on the sofa during our third hour of watching *Superstars of Science*, I saw a text bubble pop up on her phone screen that said:

Dad: OK hang in there. I'll come get you.

I didn't know what she had texted her dad before that, but I could imagine. One thing Jenna and I had in common: she had about as much fun around me as I did around her.

Dad stayed home with me the next day, but Rhoda still came in the afternoon.

When she read my notes in the Important Jar, she gave me a big hug.

"I know this is really hard, Elf. Some things are so hard that it's tough to know what to say to make it seem better.

All I can tell you is that your parents are going to do everything in their power to make this right."

"That's the thing, though," I said. "Everything in *their* power is a lot less than everything in Colton's family's power. And the school's power. So it doesn't really matter."

"*Urft,*" Rhoda said. "Well, sometimes the world surprises you in good ways too. We'll just have to see. On to a more fun topic, though: Did you and Jenna have a blast last night?"

I caught the twinkle in Rhoda's eye and socked her with a throw pillow. She reached out and messed up my hair.

"Come on, kiddo. Let's make some chocolate turtle brownies."

• • •

For the next week, I had to spend mornings at the library with Dad. The town library was usually one of my favorite places. Dad had worked there since before I was born, so everyone on the staff knew me. I was allowed to go behind the circulation desk and into the offices, and I knew where Dad's secret stash of lollipops was. Besides, it was a quiet building with rows and rows of books. What wasn't to like?

But not even the library felt fun now. Dad was in charge of a big reorganization they were doing, and he was always in serious work mode. Ms. Nudler, the children's librarian, was busy with toddler story time every day. And worst of all, I knew Dad's coworkers had heard my Hampshire story, because they looked at me with pitying faces and sad little smiles every time they saw me. It was humiliating. Every day I counted the minutes until Rhoda would finish her classes for the day and come rescue me.

The only thing I really ever felt like doing was baking. In addition to turtle brownies, over the next few days we made banana bread, orange-cranberry muffins, and even a gingerbread house. ("Why not?" Rhoda said. "We'll perfect our technique before Christmas.")

My least favorite part of baking was cleanup, but I told Rhoda I could be in charge of it for now. It was her least favorite part too. When I said I would take care of all the dishes, she said, "Woot! In that case, we can make anything you want!" She was also pretty tired; she said nursing school was still knocking her out.

I thought about what Sierra and Colton and all the other kids at Hampshire might be doing in those same moments. As I dried our whisks and spatulas, were they putting away expensive test tubes and beakers? Maybe talking about the amazing presentation they'd seen that day in their planetarium? Feeding snacks to the falcon? Making plans to hang out together after school? What was life like for kids at Hampshire? I wondered if I'd ever know.

CHAPTER 16

By Friday of that week, I was completely miserable. I couldn't bear to think about the following Tuesday, the first day of school at Cottonwood. I started wondering if there was a way I could actually slow down time by taking as long as possible to do each thing I did. I got out of bed and put my feet on the floor one toe at a time. I tried pouring my cereal into the bowl from the box one flake at a time. I set a timer and brushed my teeth for a full two minutes.

"Elfie, I'm going to be late for work!" Dad did not want the morning to go as slowly as I did. So I waited until we were at the library and practiced slowing down time there. Dad asked me to clear out the book return bins outside the building, and I made twenty-two trips, carrying the books one at a time from the bins to the circulation desk. (Dad was helping a library patron with a research project, so he didn't notice my twenty-two trips; otherwise he probably would have put a stop to that too.)

I sorted the Legos in the children's department by color, straightened the stack of scrap paper by the card catalog computer, and had just started a one-thousand-piece puzzle in the reading room when Rhoda arrived to pick me up. I couldn't believe she was there already; had doing all those things actually sped time up instead? *Urft.*

Dad was even more excited than usual to see Rhoda; I figured he was ready to unload me onto another adult. Rhoda seemed a little off too; she had a different kind of energy today.

"Hi, Elfie! Are you ready to go?" she said when she found me in the reading room. "We need to move fast!"

"Okay, let me just put away this puzzle."

Dad zipped over and shooed me from the table. "No, no, I'll take care of that later. Come on, I'll walk you guys out!"

Sheesh. He really was eager to get rid of me.

Dad and Rhoda were about ten steps ahead of me in the parking lot. I was still trying to get my sweater tied around my waist when they reached the car. Then the scene got even weirder: Mom was there.

"What's going on?" They all had goofy smiles on their faces. It was making me nervous.

"I came over here on my lunch break," Mom said. "I didn't want to miss Rhoda's surprise."

"Well, it's not really *my* surprise," Rhoda said.

"It was your idea, though!" Dad said.

"But you guys had to give it a thumbs-up!" Rhoda said. All three of them were laughing and smiling. Rhoda was positively bouncing on her toes. It was making me feel like my head was about to explode.

"WOULD SOMEONE PLEASE TELL *ME* WHAT THE SURPRISE IS?!" I yelled.

"Right, right, okay," Rhoda said. She opened the back door of her car and pulled out a big shoebox, like the kind boots would come in. Surely they weren't this excited about boots? And they wouldn't be giving me boots in August? Then I noticed there were holes in the box lid.

I experienced a chilling moment during which I was convinced there could only be one thing in the box: an earthworm habitat. I had said that I wanted one for years, and all three of these adults had always said that was a terrible idea because they knew I was afraid of bugs. "No, earthworms are different," I'd insisted. "I know I can care for them," I'd promised. Now they were calling my bluff. What had I been thinking? Why in the world would I want a glass case full of worms? I would never sleep again.

Just as I was thinking this, Mom took the box from Rhoda and held it closer to my face.

"Go on, open it!"

But at that second, the box lid started to lift on its own.

And all I could think was *Oh no, oh no, oh no, it's a giant earthworm capable of opening boxes.*

I screamed.

"Elfie, what is the matter with you?" Mom said. "You're going to scare him!"

Him? The giant earthworm was a boy? That couldn't be.

"Earthworms are actually both male and female," I said, backing away from the box.

"You think this is an earthworm?" Rhoda was laughing so hard, she could barely talk. "You goofball. Come here."

She lifted the lid, and I stepped slowly back toward the box. Inside was not a giant earthworm, or even a small earthworm. Instead, climbing up the side of the box and peering over the edge was the softest, most beautiful tiny gray kitten I'd ever seen. He boosted himself up so that we came face to face and looked in each other's eyes.

"Surprise!" Dad said.

"This is for me?" I'd never asked for a cat. It had never even occurred to me. Cute furry pets just seemed like something other people had, something Mom and Dad would say we were too busy for, or that they didn't want to spend the money on. They certainly never seemed that excited about Jenna's dog, Larry, when he came over. But maybe they would be different with a cat.

"I thought he might cheer you up," Rhoda said. "I can't believe you thought this little goober was going to be a worm."

I couldn't speak, but I nodded. When I found my voice, I said, "Thank you. And I think that's what we should name him."

"What? Worm?"

I laughed. "No, Goober! It's another word for a peanut, right?"

Rhoda nodded. "I think so."

"Well, he's so little," I said. "He seems just like a Goober."

I picked up Goober and stroked him behind the ears. Forget making things go slower; if I could have stopped time forever right in that moment, I would have.

CHAPTER 17

Goober slept in my room that night. To be more precise,
I should say that he *stayed* in my room that night. He
didn't sleep much, and as a result, neither did I.

At first, I didn't want to sleep anyway. I couldn't stop
holding Goober, scratching behind his ears, and just looking at him. I didn't even mind cleaning his poop off the rug
(although I did start trying to train him to use his litter box
right away). I couldn't believe he was mine.

Around ten o'clock, I started feeling sleepy, so I put Goober in his box. Rhoda and I had turned it into a cozy little
kitten apartment with an old baby blanket on the bottom
and a soft cat toy in the corner. I put the box on the floor
beside my bed.

When I turned out the light and closed my eyes, I heard
a scratching sound. Then a little mew. I turned to lie on my

side and face the wall. Another scratch. Another mew. I put my pillow over my head, but it seemed like the mewing got even louder. It was the most pitiful sound in the world.

My overhead light turned on. I lifted the pillow to see Dad standing in my bedroom doorway.

"How's it going in here?"

"Not so good. I don't think he's very tired."

"We could leave him downstairs, you know. We'd put a gate in the kitchen doorway so he wouldn't escape. It might be good for him to learn to sleep on his own."

"No, I couldn't do that!" I said. "It's cruel."

"I don't think so," Dad said. "Besides, it worked for you."

"What do you mean?"

"When you were a baby. You only wanted to sleep with Mom and me, and we had to help you break the habit."

"You made me sleep in the kitchen?!"

Dad laughed. "No, but we set you up in your own room, and we didn't run to you every time you fussed. It's called letting the baby cry it out. Lots of parents do it. Eventually you became a great sleeper."

"That sounds terrible. I'm not going to let Goober cry it out."

"Suit yourself," Dad said. "But I'm going to close both of our bedroom doors so Mom and I don't have to hear it." He leaned over and kissed the top of my head. "Good night, Elf."

Hmph. Was that why I wasn't very good at making friends? Because Mom and Dad trained me to like being alone when I was a baby?

Goober mewed again. I scooped him out of his box, put him on top of my comforter, and lay back down. But I guess that still wasn't close enough for him, because he burrowed slightly under the covers and curled up beside my shoulder.

"Good night, Goober," I whispered. "You can sleep with me whenever you want."

He didn't mew once until the morning.

. . .

Goober made that weekend a lot more fun. Maybe too much fun; the next few days went so quickly that before I knew it, it was Monday night, and time to get my things ready for my first day back at Cottonwood the next morning. It was First-Day-of-School Eve. First-Day-of-School Eve used to be one of my favorite days of the year. By then we'd have found out who our new teachers would be, and I'd spend the day rereading the teacher's welcome letter, reviewing my supply checklist, and resharpening my pencils.

Not this year, though. When a letter arrived from Cottonwood Elementary this afternoon, my heart sank. Usually I'd rip open the envelope because I couldn't wait to find out who my new teacher would be. This time I pulled the mail out of the mailbox, glanced at the top letter (which happened to be the one from Cottonwood), sighed deeply, and dropped all the mail onto the kitchen table. I took Goober into the living room and snuggled him to my chest as I started an episode of *Superstars of Science.*

Rhoda put down her keys and her backpack and walked over to the table.

"Hey, Elf, did you see this? I think it's your teacher letter!"

"Yes, I saw it," I said.

"Aren't you going to open it? Come on, let's find out who you got!"

"You can open it."

"Are you serious?" Rhoda was so surprised that her voice got squeaky on the word *serious.* "You never let anyone else open this letter."

"You don't have to open it if you don't want to," I said. "Technically, it's addressed to Mom and Dad. They can open it when they get home. Maybe it's not even the letter about my teacher. Maybe it's a letter saying they've learned I'm a criminal, and I'm not welcome at that school either."

Rhoda came in and gave the top of my head a sturdy *tap* with the letter.

"You are a goofball. But it makes sense that you're not excited," she said, sitting beside Goober and me on the sofa. "I know this year feels like it will be different from the others."

"No, it doesn't, actually. It feels like it will be exactly the same. Another year of school with rowdy lunches and broken science equipment and crowded classrooms and Jenna and other kids who don't like me. What doesn't make sense is that I got excited for the teacher letter all the other years. I hate Cottonwood."

"You know," Rhoda said, "*I* am a graduate of Cottonwood Elementary School. And I don't think I turned out so bad."

"That's because you're perfect," I said. "You're smart *and* funny, *and* everyone likes you. You know how to talk to every kind of person."

"Hmm," Rhoda said. "You make some excellent points. I *am* perfect. In fact, now that I think about it, I don't know why I ever bothered going to school at all."

"Very funny."

"Yes, we've already established that being funny is part of my perfection," Rhoda said. "Okay, well, if you aren't going to open this envelope, I will."

"Go ahead."

Rhoda slipped her index finger under the envelope flap and slid it open. She took out the letter inside and unfolded it; it looked like there were two pages.

"Mm-hmm. Mm-hmm," Rhoda murmured as she read. "Oh, interesting. Whoa! That's really cool!"

"I know what you're doing."

"What am I doing?" Rhoda acted confused. "I'm reading a letter."

"You're trying to get me to ask you what it says."

"No, I'm not. *I'm* just very interested in what it says. At least one of us is curious about your new teacher."

I went back to watching my show. I knew the game Rhoda was playing, and I had no interest in going along with it.

• • •

Later that night, after Rhoda had gone home, and while Dad was in the kitchen making dinner, I went upstairs to look for Goober's favorite cat toy: a gray felt mouse that smelled like lavender. I found it on top of my bed, sitting on a piece of paper. Two pieces of paper, actually. It was the teacher letter, on Cottonwood Elementary stationery.

I saw the teacher's name without meaning to; I couldn't help it. It was written in bold in the middle of the page:

Your fifth-grade teacher will be
Ms. Rambutan.

Ms. Rambutan? I'd never heard of her. She must be new. So she wouldn't know anything about me and what a good student I am. I supposed she would figure that out quickly enough.

I glanced at the second page. It was a letter from Ms. Rambutan.

Dear Students,

My name is Ms. Rambutan, and I will be your fifth-grade teacher this year. I know we will have many grand adventures together!

This is my first year at Cottonwood Elementary. Before this, I taught fourth grade at a school in Michigan. Since most of you have been at Cottonwood since kindergarten, I am sure you will serve as fine guides for a newcomer like myself.

I look forward to meeting you!

Sincerely,

Ms. Rambutan

I sighed. It was hard to tell much about Ms. Rambutan from her letter. She sounded eager and serious about learning, just like I used to be at the start of school. Too bad I couldn't muster the optimism to feel that way this year.

As I walked out of my room with Goober's little gray mouse, I noticed one more paper. This one was just a scrap, resting in the bottom of the Important Jar. I fished it out and read Rhoda's familiar handwriting:

I looked up the meaning of *rambutan* (scientific name: *Nephelium lappaceum*). It's an Indonesian fruit that is prickly on the outside and sweet on the inside. Kind of like you sometimes. 😉

♥, R

Rhoda was good at cheering me up. Her note in the Important Jar actually made me crack a smile. Maybe this wouldn't be so bad. . . . Rhoda was right; *she* had gone to Cottonwood, and she was one of my favorite people in the world. Besides, I would probably only have to go there for a little over a month before the Hampshire honor review board met and decided I was innocent.

I heard Mom come in the front door, and I started going downstairs to show her my letter.

"Hey, Elf," she called when she heard me coming. "Did you get your teacher letter yet? I talked to Uncle Rex; Jenna has someone named Ms. Rambutan."

And just like that, my smile evaporated.

CHAPTER 18

"If you drive me to school just this one time, I promise I'll never, ever complain about the bus again."

Dad gave me a look. "I find that very hard to believe."

"I just can't handle the bus today." What I really meant was that I couldn't handle a minute more of Jenna than was absolutely necessary. Even if my transportation to school was a flying carpet, I would say no thanks if Jenna was along for the ride. Not this morning.

Dad sighed. "Okay, get your stuff together. But this is not going to be a habit."

"Thank you, thank you, thank you, Dad. This is me being effusive!"

Dad couldn't help but smile at that. When I was littler, it used to bother my parents that I wouldn't jump up and down and get visibly excited when big things happened (when I got a telescope for my fourth birthday, for example, or when they took me to the dinosaur exhibit at the natural history museum for the first time). They said the most I would ever do is clasp my hands together and open my eyes wider.

"It just makes us wonder if you're really happy when we do these special things," Mom had said once when I clasped my hands together after seeing a meteor shower through my telescope. "I thought something like a meteor shower might make you more *effusive.*"

Even though I was little, I knew that *effusive* meant "expressing feelings of gratitude or happiness in an obvious or dramatic way." I didn't know how to be effusive. But that didn't mean I wasn't happy.

"I'm sorry, Mom," I'd said, trying to think of a way to make her feel better. "What if I just tell you? I can say 'This is me being effusive.'"

Mom and Dad thought that was an excellent way to communicate when I felt really happy, so that settled it. Since then, I try to remember to tell them I'm truly happy about something by saying "This is me being effusive." I didn't have to say it when they gave me Goober, though. On that day, they could tell how happy I was without words.

I was nervous about leaving Goober today. The vet said kittens shouldn't be alone for very long until they're at least four months old, and Goober wasn't that old yet. So Dad got special permission from his boss, the library director, to bring him to work until he was old enough to stay alone.

"He'll be like the office cat," Dad said. "As long as he be-haves himself, he'll be okay."

I still wasn't crazy about the idea of Goober being out in the world without me. I used our time in the car on the way to school to review the ground rules with Dad as I kept turning around to peek at Goober in his cat carrier in the back seat.

"Make sure he knows where his litter box is as soon as you get there. And give him snacks once in a while, but not too many. Scratch him behind his ears if he seems lonely. And whatever you do, do not take him to the children's de-partment. The toddlers who come to story time will suffo-cate him!"

"I know, I know," Dad said. "I took care of a baby once, remember? I can handle a kitten."

That reminded me. "Do *not* put him in a room by himself to 'cry it out'!"

Dad laughed. "Don't worry. I don't think my boss would let me keep him around very long if he made a ruckus like that."

He turned right, and I looked up and saw that we were pulling into the driveway in front of school. I tried to ignore the feeling of my heart dropping into my stomach by con-tinuing to focus on Goober. My voice sounded strained as I said, "And what about his favorite mouse? Dad, did you bring his mouse?"

Dad put his hand on my shoulder. "I have his mouse, Elf. He's gonna be okay. And so are you. But you do need to get out of the car now."

I nodded at Dad and he reached over and gave my arm a squeeze.

"You got this, kid," he said.

He was wrong, of course. I knew I didn't remotely "have this," if "this" was the strength to get through even another minute at Cottonwood. But somehow my arm did what it was supposed to do, and opened the door. I stepped out to face my first day back at my old school.

CHAPTER 19

When I walked into room 507, I noticed three things right away:

- A small woman with glasses and short brown hair standing at the front of the room and smiling
- On the table in front of her, a bright red fruit with long prickles (It looked kind of like a small hairy tomato, but thanks to Rhoda's note in the Important Jar, I knew exactly what it was.)
- Jenna sitting near the front of the room, laughing and talking with Esme Carter, who was two seats away from her

I knew Ms. Rambutan must be assigning seats; otherwise Jenna and Esme would certainly have chosen to sit right beside each other, and near the back, as far from the teacher as possible. I looked down and saw that the desks had numbers on them but no names.

Ms. Rambutan was carrying a big black top hat, the kind Abraham Lincoln wore. She came over with quick little steps, as though she couldn't wait to talk to me.

"Hello! I'm Ms. Rambutan."

I looked at her. I wondered if I would ever know her first name, the way students at Hampshire did with their teachers.

"And you are?"

"Elfie Oster."

"Welcome, Elfie!" She held the hat out with both hands, like it was heavy. "Please take a number!"

Oh. That's how the seats were being assigned. I fished around in the hat, hoping for a number that would put me as far as possible from Jenna and Esme.

I pulled out the number 8 . . . which, of course, was right behind Jenna in seat 4.

"Wait," I said to Ms. Rambutan. "Can I take a different number? I'd prefer to sit . . . near the back." That was the first time I'd ever uttered those words. I was usually most comfortable in front, and of course Jenna and Esme knew it.

"No, I'm sorry," said Ms. Rambutan. "No returns or exchanges! Besides, this looks like a great seat for you, near these two classmates. It will give you a chance to get to know each other."

"She's my cousin," said Jenna in a voice that sounded defeated. "We already know each other."

"Oh my goodness! Cousins!" Ms. Rambutan pumped her fist in the air as though Jenna had just said we were Olympians. "Well, then, you'll enjoy catching up! Have a seat, Elfie!"

I slid into the seat behind Jenna. She turned around and leaned over the back of her chair.

"My dad said you got a cat," she said. It sounded like an accusation.

"Yes. A kitten, actually."

"What's its name?"

"Goober."

"Is it a girl or a boy?"

"A boy."

Jenna nodded. "That's cool. You seem like a cat person."

That sounded like an accusation too. What did Jenna mean by that? How could someone *seem* like a cat person? I was about to ask her that when Elijah Harris sat down in the seat beside mine. His arm was in a sling.

"What happened to your arm?" Jenna asked.

"I fell off my bike, riding down Flood's Hill."

"How could you ride your bike down Flood's Hill?" I asked. "There are no paths there; it's only grass. And it's really steep."

Elijah shrugged. "I just ride on the grass. It's fun."

"You've never ridden a bike on Flood's Hill?" Jenna asked.

I sighed. "No, Jenna. I suppose you have?"

She nodded. "All the time. It's awesome. Feels like you're breaking the rules."

"You probably *are* breaking the rules," I said. "And in Elijah's case, also your arm."

Jenna rolled her eyes at me as Ms. Rambutan started talking.

"Good morning, fifth grade! Welcome, welcome! I know most of you already know each other, since this is your last year at Cottonwood. In fact, I just learned that we even have two students in this class who are *cousins*!" She gestured toward Jenna and me, and everyone looked at us. Jenna slunk down in her seat. I don't know why she was embarrassed; everyone already knew we were cousins.

"But since this is my first year at Cottonwood," she continued, "none of you know anything about me. So let me introduce myself. My name is Jovelyn Rambutan."

Huh. A teacher telling us her first name already. That's never happened at Cottonwood.

"My family recently moved here from Michigan. I taught fourth grade at a school there, so I'm excited to move up a grade! My husband and I have six-year-old twins, a boy and a girl. And here in front of me is one more clue about my background."

She pointed at the prickly red fruit on the front table.

"Does anyone want to guess what this is?"

I raised my hand right away, as did a few other students. Ms. Rambutan called on us one at a time, asking each of us to remind her what our names were.

"A spiky ball," Aliyah Marshall guessed.

"A strawberry with a weird fungus," said Will Haubner.

Then Ms. Rambutan called on me.

"Yes . . . and tell me your name again?"

"Elfie," I answered. "And that is a rambutan."

Esme Carter laughed. "No, that's *her name.*"

"I know," I said. "But that's also what that object is called. It's a rambutan. It's the tropical fruit of a tree with the same name, the rambutan tree. It grows in Southeast Asia."

Ms. Rambutan's eyes widened.

"Yes, that's right!" she said. "I didn't expect anyone to get it so quickly! How did you know?"

"She knows everything," Esme said.

Ms. Rambutan looked around the room as though she were waiting for someone to dispute Esme's statement. No one did.

"Well, that's very impressive, Elfie. And yes, this particular rambutan fruit came from a country in Southeast Asia called the Philippines. And that's where I come from too!"

"I thought you said you were from Michigan," said Elijah.

"Well, yes, that's true. Good listening!" Ms. Rambutan seemed a little flustered. "But I was born in the Philippines and moved here with my parents when I was a baby. I visited my aunt there this summer and brought back this fruit, which happens to share my family name."

Ms. Rambutan reached into a cabinet in the corner of the room and brought out a big canvas bag.

"I hope we try lots of new things in class this year, starting today! This bag is full of rambutans, and I'm going to give one to each of you." She walked around and put a rambutan on every desk.

"Please feel free to explore the rambutans! Feel how heavy they are, roll them around in your hands, smell them. And just call out what you notice."

People started yelling out things like "pointy," "prickly," and "smells funny but sweet." I didn't call out anything. I've never enjoyed the rare occasions when teachers ask you to call out responses rather than raise your hand. It makes the classroom very disorderly. Besides, how can I be sure the teacher knows I'm giving a correct answer in such a chaotic situation?

"Yes, yes, all good responses." Ms. Rambutan nodded. "Now, an important question: How do you think you eat them?"

No one, myself included, seemed to know the answer to this one. I knew from Rhoda's note that you *could* eat it, but how?

"Bite into it?" Will guessed.

"Ew, with all those prickles on it?" Esme said. "I dare you to try."

Since Will was exactly the kind of person who *would* eat a fruit with spikes all over it, he brought it to his mouth and tried to bite it.

"Ugh!"

Ms. Rambutan smiled. "Did that work?"

"No," Will said. "It's tough, and it tastes gross."

"So what do we know so far?" Ms. Rambutan asked. "Is this a fruit, like an apple or a strawberry, that you can just bite into?"

"No," Jenna said. "Maybe it's more like an orange. We probably have to peel it first."

Ms. Rambutan nodded again. "How would you do that? Don't answer yet . . . just start trying."

Jenna started to dig into the rambutan with her fingers. Elijah began poking his with a pencil. I didn't know what to do. I attempted to pull off the prickles one by one, but they wouldn't budge. I successfully severed some of them with my thumbnail, but that wasn't getting me any closer to the inside of the fruit. Why hadn't I looked up this fruit after I read Rhoda's note? Not that I ever could have known Ms. Rambutan would actually bring them into class, but still, I should have done more research. I wasn't used to being unprepared. I shouldn't even be here anyway. I should be at Hampshire

Academy using a high-powered microscope, not at Cottonwood trying to crack open a stupid prickly rind.

I started to feel very warm. Something wet splashed onto my rambutan, and I realized—to my horror—that it was a tear. I was crying over a tropical fruit.

Ms. Rambutan must have noticed because she came over to my desk.

"Everything okay, Elfie?" she asked.

"Yes, it's fine. Can I please go to the bathroom?"

"Of course. Would you like Jenna to go with you?"

Why in the world would I want Jenna to go with me? Oh, right, because we're cousins. Ms. Rambutan must think that means we're close.

"No. No, thank you. I won't be gone long." I didn't want Ms. Rambutan to think I was one of those students who went to the bathroom unnecessarily and wasted time there. So many other things had gone wrong this year. I needed my new teacher to like me.

"It's all right." Ms. Rambutan handed me a tissue. "Take all the time you need."

CHAPTER 20

I couldn't go into the bathroom. There were at least four girls in there, washing their hands and laughing. One of the other fifth-grade classes must have been doing an art project, because the girls had paint all over their hands.

But I knew I couldn't go back into Ms. Rambutan's room either. Not yet. I felt like I was having a hard time catching my breath. I did the only thing that made sense, even though it was something I never would have done before. I opened the back door of the school and stepped outside. As soon as I heard the door click behind me, I had a sinking feeling. I gave it a quick pull to see if it was unlocked. It was not. I slunk to the ground and leaned against one of the big windows that looked out over the playground. To get back in, I'd have to go around to the front door and ring the buzzer. Then everyone would know that I'd broken a rule and left the building without a teacher's permission. Only an hour into my first day and everything was going wrong. Maybe I'd be expelled from this school too.

The door clicked open. Great. A teacher must have discovered me already. Or maybe it was Assistant Principal Eastman or Principal Kleinhoffer, and then my expulsion would happen even faster.

I looked up. It wasn't a teacher, or Assistant Principal Eastman, or Principal Kleinhoffer. It was Jenna.

"Why are you out here?" I asked her. "Now we'll both be locked out."

"I was looking for you in the bathroom, and I saw you out here through the window." Jenna reached down, picked up a rock, and wedged it between the door and the doorframe. "There, now it won't close," she said. I wondered how she knew that trick. I had a feeling it wasn't her first time leaving the building without permission.

"Here, want one?" Jenna held something out to me. It looked like a small shiny egg.

"What is it?"

Jenna laughed. She could tell I didn't trust her.

"It's a rambutan! This is what they look like on the inside. They're actually pretty good; try it!"

"What if I'm allergic? Ms. Rambutan didn't ask any of us that."

"She actually did, after you left. And she has our medical records. You don't have any allergies anyway."

"How would I even know if I'm allergic to this? I've never been to the Philippines. Or any part of Southeast Asia."

Jenna rolled her eyes and held the fruit closer to me. "Oh, Elfie, just try it. Everyone else in the class did, and no one died."

I slowly took the rambutan from Jenna.

"Just watch out for the pit," she said.

I took a bite. Jenna was right. It did taste good, like a slightly sweet grape.

"Did Ms. Rambutan tell you to bring this to me?"

"I asked her if I could, and she said yes."

That was a surprise. "Why are you being nice to me?"

"I saw her give you a tissue; I thought you might be upset," Jenna said. "Did you cry? I've never seen you cry before."

"Of course you've seen me cry before. We've known each other since we were babies."

"You know what I mean. Baby crying isn't the same as crying now."

I shrugged. "I guess I don't get upset that often."

"Or you do . . . but you just don't cry," Jenna said.

I sighed. "Okay, thanks for the rambutan, Jenna. You can go back inside now."

"What's wrong with you?"

"I should have known you couldn't be nice to me for more than about twenty seconds before you start picking me apart."

"How was I picking you apart?"

"By saying I don't cry, like it's not normal. Then saying you know I get upset a lot anyway."

"ELFIE!" Jenna said my name so loudly that I jumped. "You might not cry much, but you sure are sensitive. I was *trying* to be nice and bring you a piece of fruit and see if you were okay, and now you're yelling at me to go back inside."

"I wasn't yelling. You're yelling."

Jenna spoke more softly. "You won't even give me a chance to help you. I don't think you realize that other people might understand how it feels to be upset about something."

"You don't have any idea what this is like," I said. "I'm not even supposed to be at this school right now."

"Okay, you're right." Jenna's voice was rising again. "I don't have any idea what *this very specific problem* is like. And I know it's not easy for you. But I have problems too, you know."

I snorted. "What problems do you have?"

"Jeez, Elfie, how self-absorbed can a person be? You're literally part of my family, and you haven't noticed what's going on?"

"What are you talking about?"

Jenna looked me squarely in the eyes. "When was the last time you saw my parents in the same room together?"

I thought about that. "I don't know; not that long ago?"

Actually, now that I thought some more, it really had been a while. In fact, I couldn't think of when Aunt Steph had last been at our house. Christmas?

"I don't know either," Jenna said. "And technically I live in the same house with both of them. But they're never together anymore. In fact, they've decided to split up. Didn't your mom tell you?"

"What? No!" I was shocked. I couldn't believe Mom hadn't said anything. "I guess she thought I had enough to worry about, what with everything that happened at Hampshire. . . ."

"Right," Jenna said. "Your world fell apart because you don't get to go to a fancy school and you're stuck at Cottonwood with losers like me."

"That's not what I said, Jenna."

"You don't have to say it, Elfie," Jenna said. "It's so obvious to everyone that that's how you feel. But maybe once in a while you should try to realize that other people have problems too. Problems that might be even bigger than yours. And life can stink for us too, even if we are just losers."

Jenna flung the door open and stomped back inside. Not until I heard the door click behind her did I remember her trick about using the rock as a doorstop. I was on my own to find a way back in.

CHAPTER 21

Mom was waiting at the corner when I got off the bus that afternoon, which was weird, because I'd been expecting Rhoda.

"How was the first day?" Mom said. She reached to take my backpack, which was also unusual. Mom was a big believer in kids carrying their own loads. Especially her own kid.

"Why are you here?" I asked her. Rhoda was supposed to meet me at the bus stop, like she did every day after school. Baking with her was the only thing I'd been looking forward to all day.

"Wow, nice to see you too." Mom gave a nervous little laugh.

"Sorry. I just mean, where's Rhoda? I thought she was coming today."

"She had a doctor's appointment."

"She didn't tell me that. She said she'd be here on my first day."

"She must have forgotten, honey; sorry. But it works out well because now *I* get to be here after your first day. Which I would love to hear all about."

"It was pretty much exactly what I expected," I said.

"Meaning what?"

"Meaning it was the same old thing. Same school. Same kids. Same noisy lunchroom and crowded bus."

"I see. Were you a lunchroom monitor today?"

"No. They aren't doing that anymore."

Mom nodded. "Did you sit with anyone at lunch?" She said that in a quieter voice, like it was a question she was afraid to ask.

"Yes. I sat with Ms. Rambutan."

"Your teacher?"

"Yes. I stayed in the classroom at lunch and peeled rambutans."

"You peeled what?"

"Rambutans."

"Wait . . . what do you mean? Isn't *your teacher* Rambutan?"

I sighed. "Yes, it's her last name, but it's also a kind of fruit. From the Philippines. Which is also where her family is from. But she grew up in Michigan."

"Wow," Mom said as she held our screen door open for me to go in ahead of her. "I have so many questions."

"Like what? You've already asked so many questions."

"Well, for starters, why were you peeling rambutans in the classroom instead of eating in the cafeteria with the other students?"

"I was . . . in the bathroom when everyone else peeled their rambutans and I missed it, so Ms. Rambutan said I could learn during lunch."

I almost told Mom I was outside during the class rambutan peeling, but I knew that would bring on a million more questions that I didn't feel like answering. I couldn't tell her that. I couldn't tell her I had a fight with Jenna. Or that I got locked out of school and slipped back in when one of the custodians opened the door to empty a recycling bin.

I also couldn't tell Mom that at lunchtime, I went to the cafeteria and only got as far as the front entrance. I couldn't tell her that I took one look at the room full of happy kids sitting together laughing and eating, and knew I didn't belong there. I couldn't tell her that Ms. Rambutan saw me sitting on a bench outside the principal's office, where I was sneaking bites of my turkey sandwich out of my backpack, since it was against the rules to eat in the hallway. And that she invited me to eat in her room so she could teach me what I missed about peeling rambutans. I couldn't tell Mom all those things because it would make her worry about me even more than she already did.

"So did you hang out with any other kids?"

I knew she desperately wanted me to say yes. And then it occurred to me that there *had* been another kid in Ms. Rambutan's room.

"Oh yeah, Will was there."

"Will Haubner?"

"Yeah. He was helping with rambutan cleanup."

Mom was familiar with my opinions about Will Haubner. He had been in my class every single year since kindergarten. He was probably one of the smartest kids in our grade (other than me), and he had the potential to be a very good student. He always knew the right answers to the teachers' questions, and he would ask them questions of his own that made them nod and say things like "Ooh, I like the way you're thinking!" or "Hmm, I'll have to get back to you on that one."

So you'd think that Will and I might be friends. But you would be wrong. Will was loud. He talked loudly. He laughed loudly. He even whispered loudly. He was also very emotional and made long speeches about things like animal rights and the importance of composting. His grades were not nearly as good as they could have been because he rarely turned in his homework. And he usually chatted or sang throughout independent work, as well as during group projects (so of course I always tried to avoid being in his group).

He didn't believe in tests. I know this because before most of our tests he would announce, "I don't believe in tests!" He was, in short, not my kind of person.

The one class Will reliably performed well in was music. He was the star of every school play, and he had all the solos in chorus. Ms. Dubois, the music teacher, said he had "the voice of an angel."

And of course, *of course,* Will had Ms. Rambutan this year too. "Well, it's no surprise that he's in your class," Mom said. "I guess some things never change! Was he helping with cleanup today out of the goodness of his heart, or was it a punishment for something? It's hard to know with Will."

"He volunteered," I said. "But he was also the one who made the biggest mess because he was using the rambutan peels as finger puppets and pretending they were in a rock band. Then he gave the puppets haircuts, and there were rambutan prickles all over the floor."

"I see. Remind me to look up a picture of a rambutan later; I'm having a hard time envisioning all this."

"Okay. Are you done with your questions?"

"Yes, no more questions for now. But I do want to talk to you about something."

I followed Mom through the front door and kicked off my sneakers. "Okay, I want to talk to you about something too. And I think it's the same thing you want to talk to me about, and I don't know why we haven't talked about it already."

Mom looked confused. "Okay . . . you go first. What do you think we want to talk about?"

"Why didn't you tell me Uncle Rex and Aunt Steph were splitting up?"

Now Mom looked surprised. "You know about that?"

"Yes. Jenna told me today. Why didn't you tell me? That seems like something I should have known."

Mom sat down at the kitchen table and patted the spot across from her, indicating that I should have a seat.

"I didn't know how much Jenna knew. This has all been pretty sudden."

"Jenna said she can't remember the last time they were in the house together. That doesn't sound sudden."

"It's complicated, Elf. Dad and I knew that Uncle Rex and Aunt Steph have been apart a lot. At first we just thought it was because of her work schedule, and him being busy with his band. When we started to wonder if there was more of a problem, we didn't want to say anything. Then Uncle Rex confirmed it for us about a week ago."

"You've known for a week and you didn't tell me?"

"Like I said, we didn't want to tell you anything until we knew they'd talked to Jenna. I'm surprised he didn't tell me that they did that; maybe it just happened yesterday."

"Well, I had no idea, and Jenna seemed mad about it today. Like I should have figured it out on my own or something."

"I'm sorry, honey; I'm sure she's having a hard time. This is a lot for her to process. I wouldn't take it personally."

I shrugged. It's not like Jenna and I usually got along all that great anyway.

"Well, I guess you've figured out by now that that wasn't what I wanted to talk to you about." Mom started straightening and restacking the napkins in the napkin holder, even though they were already in perfect order.

"So what is it?" I asked. And then I realized . . . she must have heard something from Hampshire Academy already. They must have said I'm expelled for good. "You talked to the Hampshire honor code board, didn't you? They aren't going to let me back. Colton told his dad I was a thief, and they won't even listen to my side, will they?"

Mom looked surprised again. "No, no, honey; gosh, I hadn't even been thinking about that."

How was that possible? I thought about it all the time.

"The honor code board still isn't meeting until October, and we'll make your case to them then. No, Elf, this is something different. This is about Rhoda."

I didn't like the way Mom's voice sounded.

"What about Rhoda? Is she quitting? Did she get a job as a nurse already?"

"No, she's not quitting, but she will be taking some time off. And she's going to have to take time off nursing school for a while too."

"Why? Where's she going?"

"She's not going anywhere, but she's had some bad news. Rhoda has cancer, honey."

That sentence sounded all wrong to my ears. Mom must be confused, or maybe I heard her wrong. *Cancer* was a word that I'd only ever heard in stories about grandparents and great-uncles and great-aunts, not young people like Rhoda.

Mom kept talking, and the words didn't sound any less strange. "Her doctors caught it in a very early stage, which is a good thing."

"So what now? What are they going to do about it?"

"Well, luckily there is a treatment that is usually very effective against the type of cancer Rhoda has. It's called chemotherapy."

"I know what chemotherapy is." I had seen an episode of *Superstars of Science* about it. Then I remembered one of the worst things about it. "It will make her lose her hair!" I pictured all of Rhoda's beautiful curly dark hair falling from her head. I squeezed my eyes closed to try to make the image go away.

When I opened them, Mom was nodding and had reached out to hold on to my arm. "That's likely," she said. "It's very powerful medicine, with very strong side effects, like hair loss. It will probably also make Rhoda feel really tired, and likely nauseous too."

"It sounds terrible. Medicine that makes you sick."

"I know. But it's also very good at zapping the cancer. And Rhoda's doctors are optimistic that this will work well for her. They want her to start next week."

I had to ask the question that scared me most. "Is Rhoda going to die?"

"I wish I knew the answer to that, Elf." Mom's grasp on my arm tightened a little. "She says her doctors are hopeful; Rhoda is young and strong, and has always taken good care of herself. But it is a serious disease, so they have to take it seriously."

I sagged back in my chair. "When can I see her?"

"Whenever you want. I told her that I'd give you the news, but we can visit her tomorrow, if you'd like."

The next question that came into my head was selfish, but I couldn't help it.

"Who's going to take care of me after school?"

"I've already talked to Keisha about working from home for a while, and she says it's fine. We're going to continue to pay Rhoda's salary while she's going through treatment, so we can't really afford to hire another babysitter."

It was so weird to think of afternoons with no Rhoda. I rested my head on the table. Mom brushed her fingers through my hair. It felt nice, but there was only one thing that I really wanted at that moment.

"Is Dad coming home soon? I need to see Goober."

CHAPTER 22

Dad got home about twenty minutes later. He was being cheerful and had lots of stories about Goober's first full day at the library. "He was a good little coworker!" he said. "He likes sitting on top of my file cabinet, he used his litter box every time, and I only had to tell him once not to eat Janet's spider plant."

I didn't say anything in response; I couldn't find my voice. I just reached out and took Goober from him and nuzzled my face against his furry neck.

"How was the first day?" Dad asked, sounding hesitant as he looked over at Mom.

"It sounds like it was okay," Mom said, "but I just told her about Rhoda."

"Oh, Elf." Dad scratched the back of my head the same way he rubbed Goober behind the ears. "This is tough news, I know."

"I'm going to do my homework now." I held Goober in one hand, grabbed my backpack with the other, and went up the stairs to my room. Out of habit, I looked at the Important Jar right away, but of course it was empty. Rhoda hadn't been here without me since last week.

I took a little square of green paper from the pad on my desk and sat down to write something to put in the jar for Rhoda. But what do you say to your best friend who has cancer? Nothing had ever prepared me for what to write at a time like this. I slid the green paper aside and pulled out my homework instead.

Ms. Rambutan had given us an introduction page to fill out, the way teachers usually did on the first day of school. At first glance, it really seemed like something that was more appropriate for second grade than fifth; I wondered if teachers in Michigan went easier on their students. I knew this certainly was not the sort of thing they would do on the first day of school at Hampshire Academy. I sighed and read the sections of the page in more detail.

Once I looked closely, though, I could see this wasn't like the "All About Me" pages we had to fill out when we were younger. Those had basic questions like *How many brothers and sisters do you have? What is your favorite color? What's your favorite food? Do you have any pets?* The page always included boxes where you could draw pictures of your answers if you didn't know how to write or spell yet. Since I already knew how to spell and write by the time I started kindergarten, I didn't waste time with the pictures. Besides, I didn't have brothers, sisters, or pets to draw. This year would have been the first time I could have done that, but there was no question about pets this time.

In fact, Ms. Rambutan's page wasn't actually even called "All About Me." It was called "Character Study: Yourself," and instead of simple questions with boxes for pictures, the questions were things like *What are you secretly afraid of? If you could change something about yourself, what would it be? If you could only eat one meal every day for the rest of your life, what would you have?* There were lines for our answers after each one.

I decided to start with the easy ones. This was not my typical approach; I usually found it best to answer test questions in order, the way they were presented to me. Even if a more challenging question was first, I always assumed that the test designer had a reason for the sequence they chose.

But this was not a test; this was a get-to-know-you page, I reasoned. And the first question was *What are you secretly afraid of?* . . . How was I going to answer that? If it was a secret, why would I share it with Ms. Rambutan, a person I'd just met? Even thinking about my answers and keeping them to myself was stressful. . . . What *was* I secretly afraid of? Never being allowed to return to Hampshire Academy? Never making real friends my own age? And worst of all, my newest fear: Rhoda dying. How could I share any of that with Ms. Rambutan? I shook my head fast to try to get the terrible thoughts out and moved on to the next question:

When were you most worried?

Well, that one was no good either. If I was being honest, I was most worried the moment that Headmaster Mulligan interrogated me about Colton's phone and expelled me from Hampshire Academy. Or at least that's what I would have said this morning. But now that moment didn't seem so bad compared to Mom telling me Rhoda has cancer. *Right now,* I thought. *Right now, worrying about Rhoda, is the most worried I've ever been.*

I shook my head again and moved on to the next question:

If you could only eat one meal every day for the rest of your life, what would you have?

Okay, that one was easy: "Mugsy's chocolate chip pancakes."

Moving on:

What frustrates you most in school?

I decided to keep that answer simple: "Group projects." Maybe Ms. Rambutan would have mercy on me and not make us do any this year.

What was a time you felt proud of yourself?

The day I found out I'd been accepted to Hampshire Academy was the most proud I'd ever felt. But how could

I write about that now? The thing that had made me feel proudest was now the thing that made me feel the most shame. I decided to make up a less complicated answer for that one: "Getting straight A's in fourth grade." The truth was, that wasn't really such a big deal to me. Getting perfect grades was what I'd always done. Perfection was more something that I just expected of myself than something that made me feel especially proud. But Ms. Rambutan didn't need to know that.

Next question: *What's something that makes you laugh?*

I put my pencil down and stretched, thinking. What made me laugh? The way Rhoda said *urft* about frustrating things made me smile, but did that really make me laugh? Rhoda's stories about her family made me laugh . . . her sister was klutzy and her mom always used the wrong words for things (like *vanilla abstract* instead of *vanilla extract*). But thinking about Rhoda's family and what they must be going through right now just made me feel scared again, and definitely not like laughing.

I tried to focus on the question. What was something I thought was funny? My mind flashed to Will in class today, using the rambutan rinds as finger puppets. I hadn't laughed at the time—I would never encourage such behavior in school—but now that I thought about it, it *was* pretty funny. Remembering the different goofy voices he'd given them and the way he pretended his pencil was their microphone stand,

I let slip a giggle. But I couldn't give that answer here; I didn't want Ms. Rambutan to think I was disrespectful like Will.

As I continued thinking, Goober jumped up onto my desk. It was an impressive feat for him; I had never seen him jump so high before.

"Whoa, Goober, well done!" I said. "That was quite a leap!"

If Goober cared that I was proud of him, he didn't show it. In fact, he turned, looked me straight in the eyes, and swatted my pencil off the table. Unlike me, Goober definitely didn't care about breaking the rules.

"Hey, Goober, I was using that!" But even while I was reprimanding him, I couldn't help but laugh. Then I knew I had my answer.

Under *What's something that makes you laugh?* I wrote: "My kitten, Goober, when he's being naughty." There. Even though the "Character Study" page didn't include any questions about pets, I'd found a way to mention Goober. Which was good, because he was beginning to feel like something that was very important in my life.

Suddenly I had no interest in doing my homework. That was a first for me.

I walked downstairs and stood behind Mom at her computer.

"I want to see Rhoda," I said. "And I want to bring Goober with me."

"I know you're eager to see her, honey. First thing after school tomorrow."

"No, I want to go now. Right now."

Mom looked surprised. It wasn't often that I made demands like that. I was usually a reasonable person. But I wasn't feeling very reasonable today.

Mom looked at her computer screen for a second. Then she turned back to me.

"Okay, let me text Rhoda. If she's available, we'll go see her."

Ten minutes later, we were on our way to see Rhoda at her mom's house. Rhoda had her own apartment above a flower shop in town, but a couple of times each week, she went to the house she grew up in to have dinner with her mom, Betty, and her younger sister, Vanessa. Rhoda always said her mom made the best lasagna, and that it was her favorite comfort food. When I asked Rhoda what that meant, she said it was food that felt like a hug. I understood. That was how I felt about the chocolate chip pancakes at Mugsy's.

Betty and Vanessa lived on a busy street where the houses were close together. Rhoda said when she was a kid, she could open her bedroom window and easily toss things to her friend Jolie, who lived next door. They would trade T-shirts, lipsticks, and even books that way. On my street, the yards were bigger and the houses were farther apart. I couldn't imagine having that kind of neighborhood, or that kind of friendship.

Betty must have seen us coming, because she opened the door as soon as my foot touched the front stoop.

"So good to see you! Oh, and you brought Goober, the famous kitten! Come here, Elfie girl; I need a hug."

"Ma, she doesn't have to hug you." I heard Rhoda's voice coming from inside. It was reassuring to hear her sounding the way she always sounded, calling her mother Ma.

"It's okay," I called back, handing Goober to Mom in preparation for the hug. Rhoda knew I did not usually like giving hugs. At all. They seemed so unnecessary and invasive. But it really was okay with me this time. Maybe I needed a hug too. And I had to admit, Betty was pretty good at it; this is sort of embarrassing and I would never say it out loud, but with Betty's giant chest, soft round belly, and apron that smelled of flour and cinnamon, she was a perfect hugger. Hugging Betty was like hugging a pile of pillows.

Mom must have felt the same way, because when Betty was done hugging me, Mom handed Goober back and hugged her for a really long time. They were still hugging when Rhoda waved me in from the kitchen. I heard one of them sniffle.

"Come here, Elf. You have to taste Betty's sauce." I always liked the way Rhoda referred to her mom as Betty (instead

123

of "my mom") when she talked to other people about her. I couldn't imagine calling my mom Justine when I told stories about her.

"Ooh, you brought Goober!" Rhoda squealed when I walked into the kitchen. Vanessa was there too, peeling a carrot. "Hey, Elfie!" Vanessa gave me a little wave with the vegetable peeler. Vanessa was the prettiest person I had ever seen in real life. She had really dark hair, and the style was always different. The last time I'd seen her, it was wavy and past her shoulders like Rhoda's; today it was really, really short and a bit spiky. I think it was what Mom would call a "pixie cut," and it actually made Vanessa look like a magical pixie. It would have made me look like a chimney sweep's broom.

"Hello, baby furball!" Rhoda scratched Goober behind the ear with one hand, and with the other she dipped a chunk of bread into a pot on the stove and brought it out, covered in red sauce. "Trade you the bread for the kitten?" she said. I took the bread and handed her Goober to nuzzle.

"It's really hot, so give it a minute. You might want to blow on it first."

I knew how good Betty's spaghetti sauce always tasted. Sweet and salty and garlicky all at the same time. And it smelled amazing. But I couldn't catch my breath enough to blow on it. I held on to the bread and looked up at Rhoda. Our eyes met, and I started to cry. I couldn't stop myself.

What was wrong with me? I never used to cry, and now it seemed like it was happening all the time.

Rhoda took the bread from me and set it on a plate. She put her hands on my shoulders. "Hug?" she asked, tilting her head a bit.

I nodded and she pulled me in. She was thinner and less curvy than her ma was, but it was still a perfect hug. It was Rhoda.

CHAPTER 23

Mom and I didn't talk much on the ride home. I was looking out the window, and Mom kept making little burping sounds and saying, "Excuse me! That's not bad manners; that's good sauce!" (It's a joke she stole from my grandfather, who always burps and says, "That's not bad manners; that's good beer!")

As we pulled onto our street, Mom said, "I'm glad we went over there, Elf. Thank you for suggesting it."

"You're welcome."

She parked in our driveway and looked over at me. "Did you and Rhoda have a good talk?" While Rhoda and I were in the kitchen, Mom had hung back and talked to Betty. I think she knew I needed time on my own with her.

"I guess. She seems okay, doesn't she?"

"She does," Mom agreed. "This won't be easy, but Rhoda's a tough bird. And I'm glad she has her family to help her."

"She said her mom will take her to her chemotherapy appointments."

Mom nodded. "Yes, Betty told me that too. They're letting her adjust her schedule at the nursing home on the days Rhoda has her chemo." Betty was an activities director for old people; she taught exercise classes and played bingo with them.

"Can we go with Rhoda on some of her chemotherapy days? She said she'll have to sit by herself for hours."

"Not by herself; Betty will be with her. I think Vanessa is going sometimes too."

"Okay, but I bet they'll get bored of each other. Maybe Betty would want company too."

"Are you saying people get bored being around their mothers for too long?" Mom smiled. "Surely you would never get bored of *me*!"

"You know what I mean. Can't we please go?"

"I'll have to think about that, Elf," Mom said. "Chemotherapy really weakens people; it might be hard for you to see Rhoda like that."

"I don't care; I can handle it."

"I said I'd think about it. I'll let you know, okay?"

"Okay." Unlike some adults, when Mom said "I'll think about it," she didn't always mean no. Sometimes, but not always.

Mom took the keys out of the ignition and opened her car door. "Did you finish your homework?"

My character study. *Urft.*

"Almost."

"Okay, well, scoot up and finish it now," she said as she opened the front door. "It's getting late."

Up in my room, I put Goober in his litter box (just in case he had to go) and sat down at my desk.

There were still three unanswered questions on my character study. I was so tired. I decided to just respond with the first things that popped into my head.

What are you secretly afraid of?

Answer: Something terrible happening to someone I love. Also, bugs.

When were you most worried?

Answer: When I found out that someone I love has cancer.

If you could change something about yourself, what would it be?

Answer: I wish I knew how to make friends.

There. I was too tired to make up answers. Ms. Rambutan had asked for a study of my character, and now she would get one. I put the paper in my backpack and got ready for bed.

CHAPTER 24

Right after taking attendance the next morning, Ms. Rambutan asked us to get out our character studies. I glanced at my answers. Suddenly I didn't feel as confident about being so honest as I had the night before. I flipped my paper facedown onto my desk, planning to quickly slide it onto Ms. Rambutan's pile as she came around to collect them. I didn't want Jenna or Esme or anyone else to see my responses.

But Ms. Rambutan had other plans.

"All right, we're going to split up into groups and share our character studies!" she announced, as though it was the best news ever. "Please count off from one to seven, and then I'll tell you where each group will gather."

Share our character studies?

Watching each student count off to see who would be in my group was a kind of stressful game, like waiting to see who would end up holding a hot potato . . . or a live grenade. Not that it mattered; there was really no one in class I wanted to talk to about my personality flaws and secret fears.

When the counting was finished, I found myself in group 4 with Will Haubner and of course . . . *of course* . . . Jenna.

I didn't listen as Ms. Rambutan explained where each group should sit. I was too busy frantically trying to erase my answers, starting with the last one about making friends.

"What are you doing?" Jenna was standing over me, with Will right behind her.

"I . . . I misspelled a word."

Jenna rolled her eyes. "You've never misspelled a word in your life. Come on." She took my paper off my desk and started to walk away with it.

"Where are you going?" I swatted at it, trying to get it back from her.

"To the hallway, like Ms. Rambutan said. Weren't you listening? That's where our group is meeting. We're supposed to trade papers and talk about them out there. Will has mine and I'm taking yours. Here, you take Will's."

Will bowed deeply and handed me his paper with a flourish. I took it and shuffled into the hall, catching the door before it closed all the way behind Jenna, who was five steps ahead of us.

Jenna was leaning against the wall and was already looking at my paper.

"Ha, group projects," she read out loud when she saw that answer. "Guess you must be feeling pretty frustrated right now, huh?"

"Can I please just have my paper back for a *second*, Jenna? I need to change something really quick."

"It's not like this is a serious *assignment*, Elfie; we're just doing a little game." She reminded me exactly of Colton Palmer, and the way he said that it didn't matter if we didn't take the marshmallow project seriously.

But then Jenna's face changed as she looked at the bottom of my paper. I hadn't had enough time to completely erase what I said about making friends; you could still read the faint letters. *Great, this is it*, I thought. *She's going to read it and laugh, then read it aloud to Will, then tell Esme and everyone else in class when we go back in.* It was the second day of school, and already I was hating a group project.

I waited for Jenna to start reading, but instead she folded my paper closed so Will couldn't see it. "You know what? This is dumb," she said, sliding the paper under her leg. "We all know each other already; let's just talk about something else while we're out here."

"Fine by me," said Will, who had been slingshotting erasers with a rubber band since we got into the hallway. "Ooh, but do read what I wrote about my secret fear." He leaned over and pointed to that line on his paper.

"Someone scooping out your kneecaps with a spoon?" I read. "That's your secret fear?"

"Yes!" He nodded vigorously. "Imagine how painful that would be! And then I wouldn't be able to ride a bike anymore, or dance in the school musicals."

Will was something else. He actually couldn't wait to share his secret fear, which turned out to be incredibly bizarre. I shook my head. Jenna laughed.

"Here's a question I've always wondered about," she said. "But it's not on the paper. If you met someone who looked, talked, and acted exactly like you, do you think you'd be friends with them?"

"You mean, if you met yourself?" I asked.

"No, not your actual self," Jenna said. "But someone who was just like you."

"How is that not yourself?" I asked. "Or at least your identical twin?" Jenna's question seemed ridiculous.

But Will was all over it. "Ooh, I love this!" he said. "So, short answer: yes, I would be friends with someone who was exactly like me. But I think I'd also be really competitive, and of course so would he, and consequently our friendship would end horribly. Possibly even violently." Will had a glint in his eye; I wonder if he was imagining scooping out his identical friend's kneecaps with a spoon.

"How about you, Elfie? Would you be friends with someone who was just like you?"

"I don't know how to answer that. It's an imaginary question."

"Can't you try, just for fun? Will knows how he'd answer it. I know what I'd say too."

Jenna was so annoying. Why was she trying to force me to answer this made-up question that wasn't even part of the homework page?

"If you know what you'd say, why don't you go first, then?" I suggested.

"Okay. If I met someone who looked, talked, and acted exactly like me, would I be friends with her? Well, first, I would notice how beautiful she was." Jenna did a dramatic flip of her hair and laughed. Will laughed too. I glowered at them.

"Just kidding, just kidding." Jenna pursed her lips and looked up, like she was thinking. "Yes, I think I would be friends with her. Because we would like talking about the same things, and watching the same shows, and doing the same stuff together. And I think we'd get to know each other pretty quickly, because we'd both be easy to talk to." Was it my imagination, or did she look at me out of the corner of her eye when she said that?

"Okay, well, that wasn't nearly as interesting as my answer," Will said. Jenna made an overly dramatic offended gasping sound.

"It's your turn, Elfie."

Will and Jenna were both staring at me, waiting for my response. I looked at the door, hoping it would open and Ms. Rambutan would come out to tell us time was up. No such luck.

I sighed. "Okay, well, I guess my answer is essentially the same as Jenna's. Of course I would get along with someone who was just like me because we would have so much in common."

"Okay, you would *get along* with her," Jenna said. "But would you really be friends? And what about the other part I said . . . would you be able to make friends with each other quickly?"

"That wasn't part of your question."

"I'm asking it now."

My face started feeling warm, and my words came out quickly. "Maybe not, Jenna. Maybe it would take forever, or maybe it would never happen at all because I'm not like you or anyone else at school, and I'm not easy to talk to, and so if I met someone just like me, we'd never be friends at all. Is that what you want me to say?"

Jenna shrugged.

"Well, this got awkward!" Will started firing erasers again. "You guys are intense. But my answer was still the most interesting."

The classroom door opened, and Ms. Rambutan peered into the hallway. "All finished?" she asked.

"Yes," Jenna said.

I didn't know what to say. I hoped Ms. Rambutan wasn't going to make us share our conversation with the class. All we knew from the assignment was that Will was afraid of having his kneecaps spooned out.

"I hope you've all gotten to know each other a little better," Ms. Rambutan said as we settled back into our seats. "I'll collect your papers so that I can read a bit about you too. We don't have time for a class share now because we have to go to music, but we'll revisit this later!"

As we filed into the hall, I couldn't help but think again about Jenna's question. *Would* I want to be friends with someone who was exactly like me? Of course I would. Right? I mean, that's one thing I'd been hoping to find at Hampshire Academy, someone like me.

Now I wondered if it would ever happen.

CHAPTER 25

Mom wasn't working when I got home. She wasn't even anywhere near her computer. When I walked in the door, I could hear her laughing, a lot. The sound was coming from the kitchen. I assumed she was on the phone with her friend Carolyn, or maybe Uncle Rex, even though he was going through a bad time. They both always made Mom laugh.

But when I walked into the kitchen, Mom wasn't on the phone. She was picking clementine oranges up off the floor and putting them in a bowl. Goober was on the counter, licking his paw.

"Oh my gosh, Elf, you have to see this!" Mom said when she saw me. "Watch what he does!" She took the clementines out of the bowl and lined them up on the counter while Goober watched. As soon as Mom was finished, Goober walked the length of the counter and swatted the oranges off, just like he had with my pencil. But this time it was one swat after another in rapid succession, like he was trying to master an obstacle course, or a carnival game. When he was finished, he didn't expect any praise, the way Larry, Jenna's dog, did when he sat on command. Goober just sat and licked his paw again. I wondered if one of the oranges was leaking and he was getting the juice off his fur.

Mom clearly thought this was superb entertainment. She was laughing so hard, tears were streaming down her cheeks. I had to admit, it was pretty funny, both Goober's trick and Mom's reaction. Dad always says Mom has a contagious laugh, and it's true. When she's laughing this much, it's hard not to laugh along with her.

I took Goober off the counter and tried to reprimand him. "Goober, we don't throw food on the floor! And now you think it makes Mom happy, so you're going to keep doing it," I said as I scratched him behind the ears.

"Oh yeah, like you rubbing his ears is some big punishment." Mom laughed again. "I can't get mad at him; he's just too cute."

I helped Mom pick up the clementines and put them back in the bowl.

"Why don't you have one of these for your after-school snack?" Mom was always trying to get me to eat more fruit.

"After they've been all over the floor? No thanks."
I opened the pantry door and took out a bag of seaweed chips instead.

"You are an interesting bird, Elfie Oster," Mom said, eyeing my snack choice. "So . . . here's a little news: we got a response from the Hampshire honor code review board today. They say they're going to start reviewing your case soon, and they want to know if we have anything to give them that supports your side of the story."

My stomach started feeling strange. "What do they mean, 'anything to give them'?" I asked. "Didn't you and Dad already write down everything I told you and send it to them right after it happened?"

"We did." Mom nodded. "But right now, it's basically a 'he said, she said' situation between you and Colton. It would help if someone else could give an account of what happened."

"Like a witness?" I asked.

Mom looked up from her phone. "Well, yes, I guess exactly like a witness. What about the other girl you mentioned at your table? What was her name?"

"Sierra," I said. "Sierra Nichols. But I barely know her; I don't know if she'd stick up for me."

"I don't know either," Mom agreed. "But there's one way to find out."

• • •

Sierra's house was in another town about twenty minutes away from ours. Even with the map app on Dad's phone giving us directions, we accidentally drove past her driveway twice. That's because her driveway was really just a narrow gravel road coming out of the woods alongside the local highway, and it was practically hidden.

When we finally made the turn, we still weren't sure we were going the right way. "It seems like we're just driving into the woods," Dad said. There were no houses anywhere. This uncertainty wasn't doing much for my nerves. When Mom had found Sierra's mom's email address in the Hampshire student directory that we'd been sent before school started, she sent her a message and asked if we could talk to Sierra about what happened on the first day of school. Sierra's mom wrote back right away, and Mom let me read her message. It said:

> Thank you for reaching out. Sierra told us all about Elfie, and we would be happy to meet you. Would you like to come to our home so we can all talk?

I had tried dissecting that email. What did it mean that Sierra had told them "all about" me? Did she say I was an interesting person? An intelligent kid? A phone thief? And did Sierra's mom sound a little odd? Why did she invite us over instead of just offering to talk on the phone? And why did she say "our home" instead of "our house"? These were some of the questions I kept asking Mom, until finally she said, "Elf, you are making me bananas. She sounds like a nice lady. She said she'd be happy to meet us, and she invited us to their house."

"Not their house. Their *home*," I reminded her.

Mom sighed. "Okay, yes, their *home*. But I don't think that's strange. And I also think they wouldn't be inviting us over—or saying they'd be happy to meet—if they really thought you were a thief. I think it's possible that Sierra might actually like you!" Mom gasped, pretending this was shocking news.

"Maybe," I said. "I guess we'll find out Saturday."

So here it was, Saturday morning, and the three of us were all on our way to meet Sierra and her family. Who, apparently, lived in a forest.

Just when I thought the gravel road would never end, Dad brought the car to a stop in front of a two-story white house with a big porch that went around the side. "Oh, I just love a wraparound porch," Mom said. It's weird sometimes, the things that grown-ups get excited about.

Mom and I got out on our side of the car, but Dad was still in the driver's seat. He wasn't getting out, although it looked like he was trying. "Eric, what are you doing?" Mom sounded a little annoyed. I think she was eager to get started on this potentially awkward meeting. I knew how she felt; the sooner it started, the sooner it could be over.

From the other side of the car, we could see Dad repeatedly opening and closing his door. He was yelling something, but we only caught bits of what he was saying. It sounded like "can't," "what the," and "coat."

"Is something wrong with your coat?" Mom yelled. Just as she started to walk around to the other side of the car to see what Dad's problem was, I heard another strange sound interspersed with his bursts of words. It sounded like a croaky sort of animal. More like a bleat than a croak, really. It sounded like a . . .

"A goat!" Mom yelled as she got to Dad's door. I raced around to where she was standing, and sure enough, there was a small but feisty brown goat trying to get into the car every time Dad opened his door.

"Yes, *goat*!" Dad yelled back. "Not *coat*! Although I think it wants to eat my coat."

He had a point. The goat was definitely lunging toward his jacket every time he opened the door to try to get out.

"What do we do? I don't know anything about goats!" Mom looked at me.

I threw my hands into the air. "Neither do I!"

I was beginning to feel panicked. I was afraid I was going to have to knock on the door of this girl I barely knew—the person who might be my ticket to get back into Hampshire Academy—and say, "I'm sorry, but there's a bit of a problem. Your goat won't let my father out of the car."

But then we were met by a sound that was even louder than the goat's bleating and Dad's muffled shouts. Ready or not, it was time to meet Sierra's family.

CHAPTER 26

"RODNEY!" yelled a woman on the porch who I assumed must be Sierra's mom. She ran down the porch steps and over to the goat, carrying a dish towel.

"Shoo! Shoo, Rodney," she hollered, swatting at the goat with her dish towel. "Bad goat!"

Rodney didn't seem very remorseful. He bleated at the woman and started nipping at her dish towel.

"*Rodney!*" she repeated in a very dismayed tone. "This is not for you. Now scat!" She pulled a handful of something that looked like granola out of her skirt pocket and flung it into the woods. Rodney bleated once more and trotted away to forage in the leaves for his snack.

"I am so very sorry," she said, wiping crumbs off her hands with the dish towel and reaching out to open the car door for Dad. "He must have gotten out of his pen. I should have made sure he was in it before you arrived."

"That's okay," Dad said, trying to stay composed and act as though goats run up to greet him everywhere he goes. But I could tell he was shaken up; Dad wasn't even really a dog person, let alone a goat guy.

The woman reached out to shake hands with Dad, then Mom. "I'm Marla Nichols, Sierra's mom," she said. She reached out for my hand next. "And you must be Elfie." I looked at her hand for a second, then reached out and let her shake mine. Shaking hands always made me feel awkward. It was something that only adults did, so when they expected a kid to do it, it seemed strange. Like they were trying to pretend we were both adults when obviously one of us was not. It felt formal, but in a fake way.

But in spite of the handshake, and the fact that she had said "our *home*" in her email, Ms. Nichols didn't really seem formal or fake. She had a bit of a Southern accent. I wondered if maybe people where she was from just spoke a little differently? But there was something about her that made me feel comfortable around her right away, and that didn't happen for me with most people.

"I'm so sorry again about Rodney," she said. "When he's not being a pest, he can be a real sweetheart. And he also helps our compost pile stay under control. We just have to keep the eggshells away from him or they'll hurt his tummy."

"Oh, that's really . . . convenient," Mom said. "We just

have a cat." I could tell she didn't really know how to react to Rodney either.

"Oh yes." Ms. Nichols nodded. "We have three of those. Well, come on in; maybe you'll meet them." She waved us toward the house. I could see Dad's eyes widen at the thought of three cats plus a goat.

But those weren't the only pets Sierra's family had. As we climbed the steps to the house, I saw an old yellow hound dog curled up in a sunny spot on the porch. It slowly opened one eye to check us out, then closed it again. Unlike Rodney, it clearly had no interest in our visit.

The next pet was another story, however. When Sierra's mom opened the front door, a small Chihuahua came charging out at us. He seemed furious to discover that visitors were on the porch.

"Oh, Edgar, settle down," Ms. Nichols said, scooping him up and carrying him into the living room, where Sierra was sitting at a corner table with a stack of books; she appeared to be doing homework. I guess students at Hampshire Academy got homework even on weekends. They were so lucky.

Two identical boys who I guessed were about eight years old were sitting on the floor playing Uno. If they noticed our arrival, they didn't show it. Neither did Sierra; she was concentrating deeply on whatever she was writing.

"Sierra, Elfie's here," Ms. Nichols said. Sierra looked up from her paper.

"Oh, hi!" she said. She actually seemed happy to see me. Or at least surprised.

"Hi," I said. I wasn't sure what to do next. Should I go over to the table? Ask what she was working on? Shake hands like her mother had? I suppressed a nervous giggle at that thought. Even *I* knew not to shake hands with someone my own age.

I guess Sierra wasn't sure what to do either, because after standing up, she just leaned against her worktable.

"Hey, watch it!" One of the boys on the floor bumped Sierra's foot with his knuckles. "You almost kicked our cards."

"I did not," Sierra said. "Besides, if you don't want anything to happen to your cards, you should play at a table, not on the floor." She looked at me and rolled her eyes.

"*You* were sitting at the table doing your super-important homework!" the boy shot back.

"We have other tables!" This time Sierra did nudge the cards with her big toe.

"*Mom!* Did you see that?" The boy looked up and seemed as outraged as if he'd been slapped.

"Okay, okay," Ms. Nichols said. "Let's give each other some space. We need to use this room anyway. Lee, pick up the cards and take them into the kitchen." The outraged boy huffed and started collecting the cards as the other boy started to slink by his mother to leave the room.

"Hang on, Curtis." Ms. Nichols stopped him and handed him the Chihuahua. "Take Edgar with you. He's being a menace today."

When the boys had cleared the room, Ms. Nichols gave a big sigh. "Sorry again that it's such chaos here. You know how Saturdays are, with everyone home."

Mom and Dad nodded, but I knew what they were thinking: our Saturdays were *nothing* like this. Saturdays with the three of us and Goober were much, much different from this scene with Sierra, her twin brothers, two dogs, and a goat. We hadn't even seen the three cats yet.

"Andy is just finishing some repairs on the chicken coop; he'll join us in a minute. Can I get you some coffee, or some lemonade? Or something else?"

Sierra's family had chickens too? And to think that the day I met her, I daydreamed about her having even an earthworm habitat.

After Sierra and her mom got coffee for the grown-ups and lemonade for Sierra and me, her dad came in and sat with us in the living room. Like Sierra's mom, he shook my hand and apologized to us about Rodney.

"Sorry I couldn't come to your rescue," he said. "I heard hollering, but I was stuck on top of the coop; I'm glad Marla got to you before Rodney ate anyone's shirt!"

Mom laughed. "So are we!" Dad looked less amused; he

pulled the zipper on his jacket up just a smidge, as if he was still trying to keep it safe from Rodney.

"So . . ." Sierra's mom sounded like she wasn't sure how to bring up the reason we were there. But Sierra jumped in.

"My mom said you guys wanted to talk to me?" she said. "About what happened on the first day of school?"

"Yes." Mom nodded. "We understand you saw what happened with Elfie and Colton, and you might be able to tell us about it?"

Dad chimed in. "We're trying to help Elfie's case with the honor code review board. They've heard her side of the story, and they've heard Colton's, but we think it might be helpful if someone else could describe what they saw." He paused. "To be honest, it seems like they believe Colton's story more right now. And his dad is on the review board."

Sierra's dad snorted. "Of course he is."

"*Andy.*" Ms. Nichols's voice had a warning tone, like she didn't want her husband to use sarcasm in front of guests. But it was already out there.

"Yes, well, we know they're pretty well connected at Hampshire," Dad said. "The library and all."

"They're *very* well connected," Mr. Nichols said. "And Sierra tells us that kid has already missed a few days of school, and the year just started. Seems like he can get away with anything."

"We don't know what's going on in their family," Ms.

Nichols said. "Maybe we should just talk about what we *do* know. That's why the Osters are here."

Mr. Nichols nodded. "Sorry. I know this school is great for Sierra, especially the science classes. That's why she went out for the scholarship to go there. But I just hope all the kids are getting a fair shake, even if their grandfathers didn't buy a building."

So Sierra got financial aid to go to Hampshire, like I did. I was surprised her dad had admitted it so soon; my parents always told me money talk was private. But I could already tell the Nichols family was pretty straightforward. I started to feel like maybe they could be on our side.

"Sierra, why don't you tell the Osters what you told us about the first day of school?" Her mom glanced at me and gave Sierra a nod.

"Well, it happened really fast. But Colton was about to cheat. Olivia, the science teacher, had told us we couldn't use anything to help with the assignment. And he took out his phone to look up ideas online. It was obviously against the rules. And then Olivia started to come over to our table, and that's when Elfie took his phone."

"Did it seem like she was *stealing* it?" Mom asked.

Sierra shook her head. "No. I understood why she did what she did. I mean, I don't know if I would have done the same thing, but Colton was making me nervous too. He was cheating. I thought we were about to get in big trouble."

"But I got in big trouble anyway," I said. It just came out without me realizing I was talking. My voice was croaky; it occurred to me that I'd barely spoken the whole time we were there.

"I know," Sierra said. "I'm sorry. I felt terrible about that. I didn't know what to do. I was afraid that if I said I'd seen you take the phone, I'd get kicked out too, for not reporting it. But I hated that they did that to you. It was awful." Now Sierra's voice sounded croaky.

"We didn't know your family, and we weren't sure exactly what had happened," Sierra's mom said. "I'm sorry we didn't speak up sooner. But when I got your email, we talked about it with Sierra, and it became clear to us that we should help however we could."

I saw Mom scrunch up her nose the way she does when she's trying not to cry. But she admitted her feelings anyway.

"Well, that almost makes me tearful," she said. "Thank you all so much." She put her hand on my knee, and I knew she wanted me to say something too.

"Right," I said. "Thank you." I wished it hadn't come out sounding forced. But I didn't know exactly what to say, or just how to tell Sierra how grateful I really was. I was starting to feel like someone at Hampshire knew I wasn't a criminal after all.

• • •

I didn't talk much on the way home. After a while, Mom looked at me in the back seat and asked what I was thinking about.

"I'm thinking about *menagerie*," I said. "The word *menagerie*."

"Oh, you mean because of all the animals at Sierra's house? They definitely have a menagerie there."

"Yes. And that's what I said to Sierra. Before we left, I told her I was glad I got to meet her menagerie. And now I'm thinking about how she didn't laugh, or tell me I was weird, or say that was a nerdy word for a kid to use."

"What did she say?" Mom asked.

"She just nodded and said I could come back and visit the menagerie whenever I wanted." I shifted my glance from the window to meet Mom's eyes in the rearview mirror.

"Would that be okay? Can we do that?"

Mom reached back and squeezed my hand. "Yes, Elf. I think that's a perfect idea."

CHAPTER 27

Ms. Rambutan was telling us a story about her *lola* in the Philippines (*lola* is how you say "grandma" in Tagalog, the language lots of people in the Philippines speak). She liked to tell us lola stories on days when we had extra time; she called it taking a brain break. "How about you take a little brain break while I tell you a story about my lola?" she'd say. I never really felt that brain breaks were necessary, but the rest of the class always cheered when she offered one, so there you had it. Majority rules.

Today's brain break story was about how Ms. Rambutan's lola used rambutans in all her cooking—rambutan salads, rambutan juice, rambutan pudding. She said that her lola made them so much that her father got sick of them.

"So even though my father's name is Mr. Rambutan, he will tell you that rambutans are his least favorite fruit! That is a great example of irony. Does anyone know what irony is?"

"Yes!" Will practically shouted. "It's what you have to do to get wrinkles out of your clothes!"

I rolled my eyes. There was no way Will didn't know the actual definition of *irony*. He was just trying to get people to laugh, and of course it worked.

Even Ms. Rambutan smiled. "No, Will, that's *ironing*. Can anyone help us with *irony*?" She wrote the word on the board.

I raised my hand. When Ms. Rambutan called on me, I said, "It's when the truth about something is the opposite of what you would expect it to be. Since your dad's last name is Rambutan, you would expect him to like that kind of fruit. The fact that he doesn't is *irony*."

"Yes, exactly, Elfie!" Ms. Rambutan smiled. "Okay, brain break is over; you may file out—quietly, please—to go to lunch!"

Ms. Rambutan stopped by my desk as people were starting to leave.

"Elfie, do you think you could stay here for a moment during lunch? I'd like to talk to you about something."

I nodded. I wondered what she wanted to talk about. Maybe she was going to recommend reinstating my Student Lunch Monitor program, and she needed to ask my permission. Or maybe she wanted my thoughts on the new math curriculum. Or to thank me for my perfect definition of *irony*. It was good to think that Ms. Rambutan might be starting to recognize what a valuable student I was; I knew it was only a matter of time.

As it turned out, Ms. Rambutan did not want to discuss any of those things.

"Thanks for staying in, Elfie," Ms. Rambutan said when the last of my classmates had filed out. "This won't take long. I wanted to talk to you about your character study."

Oh. That.

"I appreciated how honest it was. And interesting! I loved learning that your kitten makes you laugh, for example. And thank you for telling me how you feel about group projects; I will see if that's something we can make more enjoyable for you this year."

"Mm-hmm." I knew that wasn't the part Ms. Rambutan *really* wanted to talk about.

"But I would feel remiss if I didn't ask you about two things in particular," she said. "Your loved one with cancer, and also your thoughts about making friends."

Right. There it was. *Why* had I felt the need to be so honest?

"I know these are private matters, so I'll understand if you don't wish to discuss them," she said. "But I do want to give you a chance to talk if you'd like to. And I also wonder if there's anything I can do to help."

I wanted to say, "Sure, can you take away my babysitter's cancer?" But I didn't want to give Ms. Rambutan a hard time. She did seem like she wanted to help. (Plus, she was my teacher. When was I ever someone who gave teachers a hard time?)

"No one can do anything about the cancer, except maybe the doctors," I said.

Ms. Rambutan nodded. "Do you mind if I ask who the person with cancer is?"

"It's my babysitter. Rhoda." Rhoda's name stuck in my throat for a second; it was weird to be talking about her this way.

"Oh, I see," Ms. Rambutan said. Was it my imagination, or did she sound a little relieved? Like maybe she thought it wasn't such a big deal to have a babysitter with cancer, as opposed to one of your parents. She didn't get that Rhoda almost *was* like one of my parents.

"I know that must make you worry, and worrying can make it difficult to focus. If you ever feel like you're having a hard time concentrating in class, please let me know."

I almost laughed. It was a nice offer, but clearly Ms. Rambutan didn't know me very well.

"I *never* have a hard time concentrating in class," I said.

Ms. Rambutan smiled. "Okay. I can't say that surprises me. I have heard from Ms. Puckett and other teachers here that you are an excellent student."

That was good to hear. But I wondered what else Ms. Puckett and the other teachers had said about me. Mom and

Dad said that none of the teachers at Cottonwood knew the real reason I was back this year, and that they'd just told them there was a change of plans. But I wasn't so sure. Bad news always traveled fast.

Ms. Rambutan looked down at her hands for a second. "I know the other part might be even harder to talk about, but it is important. . . . Would you like to tell me more about why it's hard to make friends?"

No. No, I very much would not like to tell Ms. Rambutan why it was hard for me to make friends.

"Oh, I don't know why I wrote that," I said. "I was joking."

"Oh, I see." I could tell Ms. Rambutan didn't believe me. "I'm just curious, since I'm still getting to know everyone here. Who are some of your friends?" Nope. She definitely didn't believe me.

"Well, it's not really anyone who goes here," I said. I tried to think fast. "I mean, my friend Sierra goes to Hampshire Academy. She has a goat. And chickens." There. Maybe giving details like that would keep Ms. Rambutan from guessing that I'd only met Sierra twice in my life.

"Wow, that sounds like a fun friend to have." Ms. Rambutan smiled. But she wasn't finished.

"What about Jenna?"

"Jenna's my cousin."

"Yes, but you're the same age, so I thought perhaps you were also friends?"

"Jenna and I don't have a lot in common other than that." I wondered if Ms. Rambutan would point out that that was another example of irony, the two cousins who are always thrown together but want nothing to do with each other.

But she didn't say that. She just said, "I see. Well, thank you for filling me in, and please do let me know if I can help."

She looked at me as though she was hoping I'd say more. When that didn't happen, she patted my back and said, "Okay. You can run along to lunch."

CHAPTER 28

After my talk with Ms. Rambutan, I suddenly felt very conspicuous, and not in a good way. I was accustomed to teachers noticing me for things like cooperation, insightful answers during class discussions, and perfect scores on tests. But now I felt like Ms. Rambutan was watching me to see if I was upset about Rhoda, or group work, or not having friends. I didn't want to be noticed for those things. So I tried my best to appear content.

I hadn't gone back to her classroom at lunchtime after the first day of school anyway. On the second day of school, I'd tried offering to organize Ms. Rambutan's library or sharpen her pencils, but she'd said, "No, no, Elfie; this is your free time! Go enjoy your lunch!" Now I definitely knew not to try those tactics. I didn't want her to observe my continued friendlessness.

That created the problem of what to do during lunch,

since there were no obvious classmates for me to sit and eat with. I had asked Assistant Principal Eastman if I could start the Student Lunch Monitor program up again. At least that way I'd have an excuse to stay standing throughout lunch. But she was not interested. "Let's just see how it goes this year," she said. "Maybe your fellow students will surprise you and be on good lunchtime behavior." I nodded politely, even though I knew that was highly unlikely.

For a while, I tried walking around and pretending I was looking for something during lunchtime, taking occasional bites of my sandwich as I wandered. That was somewhat successful until one of the cafeteria staff members asked what I was looking for. When I said the first thing that popped into my head (which was "my pencil"), she said, "I'll keep an eye out for it. But you need to find a seat." I'd just nodded at her and spent the rest of lunchtime in the bathroom.

So I came up with a strategy: I knew if I could be among the first kids to reach the cafeteria, I could have my choice of tables. And the table I chose was perfect for someone dining alone. Unlike the other long cafeteria tables with benches, this one was small and square, with just two chairs. It was wedged into an alcove by the front door where there wasn't space for a long table. I knew the student body of Cottonwood Elementary was getting bigger and bigger every year, so I guess they had to fit seats wherever they could, especially for the younger grades.

But fifth grade was not quite as overcrowded, so I was able to have this table all to myself. I would sit in one chair, put my backpack in the other, and read a book or do homework as I ate. That way, if any overly concerned people such as Ms. Rambutan happened by, I hoped it would appear that I was just busy, not lonely, and perhaps even as though I was saving the other seat for someone. It was the only option I could think of.

This plan worked well until the day I was reading a biography of the mathematician Katherine Johnson, and caught a tiny movement out of the corner of my eye. I glanced at the wall beside me, and what I saw made me leap out of my chair. About a hundred ants were making their way in a long line from the ceiling to the floor, where they were swarming around a decaying grape. I recognized the ants because we'd had the same type in our kitchen a few years before. They were called pavement ants. I'd looked up their scientific name when we had them in the kitchen, and I whispered it in horror now as I scooted my chair farther from the wall.

"*Tetramorium caespitum.*"

"They'll battle to the death, you know." A voice over my shoulder made me jump. I turned and saw Will and his friend Maxine standing just behind me, eating ice cream with little flat wooden spoons.

"Who will?"

"The pavement ants. They're one of only a few ant species that will do that. Just wait and see; I bet once most of that grape is gone, they'll start killing each other over it."

"Well, I don't think we'll be here long enough for that. Lunch is over soon."

"Maybe we just don't go back to class."

I snorted. "I think Ms. Rambutan would notice that."

Will shrugged. "We could tell her we had to observe this in the name of science."

Maxine nodded. "That's true. This is very scientific." I think that was the most I'd ever heard Maxine speak off a stage. Like Will, she was in all the school plays, and she was very enthusiastic about singing, dancing, and drama. Unlike Will, she was almost completely quiet offstage. She never spoke in class unless a teacher called on her. Sometimes she didn't even speak then. Her most notable trait, apart from her interest in theater, was that she wore headbands with springy antennae on them every day. Some days they had stars on the tips; other days, pom-poms or rainbows or peace signs. It was an interesting fashion choice for such a quiet person.

The bell rang, but Will and Maxine didn't move. In fact, Will sat in the chair I'd been sitting in and slid it closer to the wall so he could examine the ants. Maxine sat across from him.

"The bell just rang," I pointed out. "We have to go back to class."

Will sighed. "Elfie, I thought you liked science."

"I do. But I also like not getting in trouble."

"Sometimes you have to chase your passion, no matter the cost," he said, and turned back toward the wall.

I looked at Maxine, hoping she'd talk some sense into Will, but she just nodded her boing-boing heart antennae in agreement with him and leaned across the table to watch the ants.

Even though I returned to class, I kept thinking about what Will had said, and I didn't report him and Maxine for staying in the cafeteria. I guess I didn't want to get in the way of them "chasing their passion." (And they didn't get in trouble after all; Ms. Rambutan just sent Elijah to retrieve them from the cafeteria when she noticed they were gone.)

I did, however, report the ants to Assistant Principal Eastman on my way to the bus lot that afternoon. She was helping a crying kindergartner who didn't know which bus to take, and she didn't seem very concerned about the ant infestation.

"Oh no, the ants are back?" she said mildly. "Okay, we'll ask the custodian to call an exterminator."

I was alarmed to hear her say the ants were *back*, which meant that they had been there before. That was news to me. I suppose in my years as student lunch monitor, I hadn't had an opportunity to closely examine the cafeteria walls.

"Well, thank you," I said. "They're especially bad by the table for two near the door."

But I'm not sure Assistant Principal Eastman heard me, because by then she was back to consoling the crying kindergartner. And in fact, the following day, the ant problem did not seem any better. If anything, it was worse.

When I got to the cafeteria, I stood staring at the wall, holding my lunch box in one hand and my Katherine Johnson biography in the other. I didn't know what to do. How could I sit at an ant-infested table?

"Whoa, they're back with a vengeance!" Will was standing behind me again. So was Maxine; today her antennae had winky-face emojis on them.

I sighed. "Yes, they certainly are."

"Hey, can we sit with you today?" Will asked. "We'll find another chair to pull over. That way we can watch the ants all through lunch."

"You *want* to sit here?" I asked. "With the ants?"

"Well, yeah, with you and the ants."

"*I* don't want to sit with the ants."

"Oh. Well, you don't have to sit with us. Or you can sit in the third chair we pull over; that one will be farther from the wall."

I weighed my options. Either I sat with Will, Maxine, and the ants at my usual little table, or I took my book and my lunch to sit at the end of one of the long tables, with a group of kids who may or may not want me there. ("May not" seemed more likely.)

"Okay," I agreed. "But definitely let me sit in the farthest chair."

Maxine spotted an extra chair behind the recycling bin and pulled it over for me, winky-face antennae bobbing the whole way. I sat in it and tucked my book under my leg; it seemed rude to read with other people at the table. Katherine Johnson would understand.

By the end of that lunch, Will had told Maxine and me enough about pavement ants that I felt a little braver about watching them closely. Some of the information I already knew, like that ants can lift twenty times their own body weight. Other bits were new to me, such as the fact that an ant colony can survive for only a few months without its queen. Pavement ants were more interesting than I'd thought. So was Will.

So when Assistant Principal Eastman spotted me across the bus parking lot and called out, "Hi, Elfie! Are those cafeteria ants still a problem?" I answered back, "No, everything's going well!" It didn't feel like a lie. Even though the ants were very much still there, they weren't bothering me anymore.

CHAPTER 29

Hi Rhoda—

I told Mom I wanted to email you before I started my homework because I have to tell you what happened today: Will finally got his wish and two of the pavement ants fought each other to the death. It was disgusting, but fascinating. They were fighting over a cracker crumb. Maxine almost cried at the end because she felt sorry for the dead ant. But Will and I explained to her that that's just how nature works.

How are things with you?

Love,

Elfie

Hi Sweet Elf!

Whoa, that is wild about the ant fight! I bet that's the only kind of fight anyone can get away with at

school. ☺ See, I told you Cottonwood isn't so bad . . .
I bet they don't have ant fights in the cafeteria at
Hampshire!

I'm glad to hear you're having fun at lunch with
Will and Maxine. You probably never thought you'd
get to be friends with Will Haubner, huh?

Things are okay here. Some good days, and some
bad, but I guess that's true for everyone. I feel like I
should warn you that next time you see me, I'll look
pretty different. Vanessa shaved my head for me.
Some people say that's the best way to deal with
your hair before you start chemotherapy; otherwise it
might fall out in clumps and look even more unusual
than a bald head. I will admit that I cried when she
first did it, but now I'm getting used to it. I don't know
if I'm ready to show it off in public, though, so I've
been wearing a baseball cap when I go outside. Oh,
and my aunt Carol got me this *really* fancy scarf that
my ma said must have cost a small fortune, so I'm
saving that to wear if I have to go somewhere nice.
I can't wait to show it to you. It has butterflies on it
(but no ants! ☺).

Go finish your homework now, but write back
when you can. Your emails are the highlight of my day!

Love,

Rhoda

Since Rhoda and I couldn't use the Important Jar to communicate now, we'd started emailing each other almost every day. I was better at email than at talking on the phone; somehow it was just easier to put what I wanted to say in writing.

Rhoda's emails were usually full of funny stories about her mom and her sister, or about something she'd read in a science magazine in her doctor's waiting room that made her think of me. But this last email was more serious; I couldn't imagine Rhoda crying, and I certainly couldn't picture her without hair. I wasn't sure how to respond to it.

I started with the less serious part:

> Hi Rhoda—
>
> Yes, I guess I'm enjoying sitting with Will and Maxine at lunch, but that's mostly because of the ants. I don't know that I'd say Will and I are "friends." He still annoys me with the way he calls out answers without raising his hand in class, and he sings to himself during writing. But he does make up adventure stories about the ants as we're watching them, so that can be entertaining. Maxine is very quiet, but nice.

I thought for a long time about what to write next. Finally I came up with this:

I'm sorry about your hair. Remember when I was little and I cut my head on my telescope, and I was upset about how the cut was still there the next day? I will always remember that you said, "Elfie, you are still Elfie, even with a cut on your head. And someday it will go away."

Well, I guess that's the best thing I can think of to say to you right now. You are still Rhoda, even without your hair. And someday it will come back.

I hope I get to see you soon.

Love,

Elfie

CHAPTER 30

To my great relief, Ms. Rambutan hadn't mentioned the character study again. The only character studies we were doing were for fictional characters in the books we were reading. We were also starting to study algebraic concepts in math, and chemical reactions in science. Ms. Rambutan made everything really interesting . . . and best of all, most of our assignments were to be completed independently.

Until the day she brought in the eggs.

"Now that we're all getting to know our classroom family, I want to talk to you about a new social studies project," Ms. Rambutan said with visible excitement as she stood beside an egg carton on her desk. "As you can see, here I have some rather ordinary eggs, although they are fresh from a local farm. They are the eggs of the *Gallus gallus domesticus*, which is the scientific name for the ordinary chicken." She looked at me, and I nodded. Ms. Rambutan had learned how important scientific names are to me.

"But these will soon be much more than ordinary eggs to you," Ms. Rambutan went on. "They will be your children! This is the first day of our egg baby project. You will be responsible for keeping these eggs safe and well cared for, just as if they were your babies.

"You'll be keeping track of your parenting adventure in a baby journal. This is where you'll write about Baby's activities, your favorite parts of being a parent, and anything you find challenging. And new parents like to take lots of pictures, so include photos or drawings too. This may sound like a lot, but don't worry; you'll be working in groups! I'm going to keep you in the same groups you did your character studies with on the second day of school."

Urft. I was going to be the parent of an egg, and I had to do this project with Will and of course—*of course*—Jenna.

The class had questions. Lots of them. Elijah: Why don't we each get our own egg? (Answer: Because raising children is ideally done by a family and a community, and part of parenting is learning to value the input of others.) Esme: Why do we have to learn about being parents when we're only in fifth grade? (Answer: Because it's never too soon to learn more about responsibility and empathy, and as the oldest students at Cottonwood, we should strive to be examples of both for the younger students.) Jenna: Shouldn't the eggs be in the refrigerator? (Answer: No, since these eggs are farm-fresh, their protective coating hasn't been washed off. So it's safe to keep them at room temperature for a week or two. But don't give your babies baths, because it will wash that coating off!) And Aliyah asked the question that was at the top of everyone's mind: What if the egg breaks? (Answer: Try your very best to keep that from happening. But if it does, it will be a chance to think about what you should have done differently.)

Ms. Rambutan had us sit with our groups, then she passed out booklets called *Caring for Your Egg Baby: A Guide for New Parents*. The first page, "Getting Started," gave a list of decisions we should make at the beginning of the project, including:

What will your egg baby's name be?

What will your egg baby look like?

Who will take your egg baby home first?

I glanced at the group beside us. Esme was standing with her arms folded and shooting desperate looks at Jenna. I was sure they both considered it a tragedy that they weren't in a group together. But Esme's groupmates, Elijah and Maxine, seemed happy enough. Maxine was even sketching an egg wearing a little outfit, complete with springy baby chick antennae.

Will noticed Jenna and me gazing at the other group and snapped his fingers to get our attention. "Guys, let's get to work. Our egg baby needs us." Jenna gave me a surprised look, and for once I could tell we were thinking the same thing: it was very unlike Will to take schoolwork so seriously.

Will wrote *name*, *looks*, and *home first* on three pieces of paper, folded them up, and put them in Jenna's pencil case. When we pulled them out, I got *looks*, Jenna got *name*, and Will got *home first*.

The baby's gender was determined when Jenna named it Linda McMuffin. McMuffin was inspired by Jenna's favorite egg breakfast. Linda is our grandma's name. "She'll be honored!" Jenna said. I wasn't so sure. Grandma Linda didn't even like eggs; she always ate oatmeal when she visited us.

It was my job to draw Linda McMuffin's face and hair. I was pleased, because this felt like an important responsibility, and I wasn't sure I trusted Jenna or Will to be in charge of our baby's looks. Art was never my greatest area of interest, but I felt confident that I could make an attractive egg.

I started with the green eyes. "Why green?" Jenna asked. I explained that it was a nice color, but also that I was inspired by Goober's green eyes. "That's not so special," Jenna said. "All cats have green eyes."

"That is patently false," I said. "Cats' eyes can be a wide array of colors."

Jenna rolled her eyes. *"Patently false,"* she repeated. "You're so weird, Elfie."

Will chimed in. "She's right. It is patently false. My cat

has orange eyes. Ooh, can Linda McMuffin's eyes be orange instead?"

I was simultaneously grateful to Will for defending me and annoyed that he was trying to take over my part of the assignment.

"I'm in charge of drawing, remember? Besides, humans don't have orange eyes."

"She's not a human; she's an egg," Will said.

"Yes, but we're supposed to be pretending she's a human baby." I couldn't believe I was having this conversation.

Will had another idea. "Ooh, I think vampires might have orange eyes! Maybe she can be an egg baby vampire. And she drinks other eggs' yolks for sustenance!"

"Our egg baby is not a vampire," I said. "She is a pretend human baby, and she is going to have green eyes because I am in charge of drawing them and I am making them green!"

Esme looked over at us from her group's table. "Jeez, relax," she said. "It's just a school project."

"Nothing is ever 'just' anything for Elfie," Jenna said. "Especially when it comes to school projects. She takes them very seriously."

Jenna said it like it was a bad thing.

"Well, maybe we *should* take this project seriously," Will said. "Linda McMuffin is our child, and only the best is good enough for her. Go ahead, Elfie, draw those green eyes. I trust you."

It was the nicest thing Will—or anyone my age—had ever said to me. I suppose it would have been appropriate to say "Thank you" in return, but I couldn't make my voice work. I just nodded, took the green marker he was holding out, and made two little dots for Linda's eyes. I added a nose and a little smile with a thin black marker, then paused, thinking what to draw next.

"Are you sure you don't want help?" Jenna asked. I could tell she didn't trust my drawing skills.

"I know what I'm doing." I picked up the orange marker and used it to give Linda wavy hair. I thought Will might like that (since he hadn't gotten his way with the orange eyes), and I was right.

"Nice!" he said. "Linda has wavy hair, like her dad. Wow, it's weird to think of myself as someone's dad."

"You aren't *really* her dad," Jenna said.

"Sure I am," Will said. "We are all Linda's co-parents, and we are raising her in what will hopefully be an amicable shared custody arrangement."

Jenna didn't have a response to that. Her cheeks turned slightly pink, and she looked down at the floor, jamming her hands into the back pockets of her jeans. I knew she was thinking about her own situation and her parents' breakup. I wondered if she would be taking turns living with Uncle Rex and Aunt Steph, the way Linda McMuffin would split time between our houses. For the first time ever, I actually felt bad for my cousin.

"Here, Jenna," I said. "Why don't you give Linda an outfit. You're good with fashion."

Jenna looked skeptical. "Are you sure? You're supposed to be in charge of this part."

"I insist."

And that is how Linda McMuffin wound up with green eyes, wavy orange hair, and a glittery silver jacket. One element for each of her three co-parents. Now if only she could survive the bus ride home.

CHAPTER 31

"Make way, make way! Linda McMuffin is coming through!" Will held his left hand far in front of him to ward off the younger kids as he, Jenna, and I made our way to the back of the bus. In his right hand, he carried Linda McMuffin.

As soon as Will sat down, he wrapped her in his scarf and cradled her like an actual baby. He barely even looked up at me when I said goodbye and got off at my stop.

Mom was working at her laptop at the kitchen table when I walked in. Goober was playing with the wire of her charger, and Mom kept trying to nudge him away.

"How was school today, Elf?"

"Okay, I guess. Except we were assigned a group project."

"Oh boy. What is it?"

"We have to take care of egg babies. Do you know what that means?"

"Yes." Mom nodded. "I've heard of schools doing this. We did something similar when I was a kid, only we used bags of flour instead of eggs. Less fragile, but much heavier. So where's your egg?"

"Oh, she's at Will's house. It was his turn to get her first. Then Jenna, then me."

"Jenna and Will are in your group?" Mom raised her eyebrows.

"Yes." I didn't say anything more. I thought maybe I would pleasantly surprise Mom by not complaining about this. At least not yet.

"Okay. Have you started working on it?"

"A little. Will and I discussed it at lunch."

"What about Jenna?"

"She came over once to ask if we needed help, but we were just setting a budget, and she said she didn't care if we did that part without her."

"Oh. What part does Jenna want to help with?"

"Picking out clothes. Will wants to do that too, so I hope they don't fight over it. It doesn't really make a difference to me. Oh, and Jenna got to name the baby. Her name is Linda McMuffin, after Jenna's favorite breakfast, and after Grandma."

Mom tilted her head to the side, like she was processing that news. "I *think* Grandma would be honored by that?" she said. "It might take a while to explain to her, though. And what about you? What part of the project do you most want to do?"

"Well, the budgeting is interesting," I said. "Babies are expensive."

Mom smiled. "That's for sure!"

"And I also told Will that I can be in charge of Linda McMuffin's education. You know, making sure she has a lot of good books, math manipulatives, and challenging puzzles. And that she is registered for an excellent preschool. He said he'll handle her cultural and arts education."

"Wow, this is a lucky egg to have such dedicated parents. I hope you're also going to make sure Linda McMuffin has time to play and have fun?"

I shrugged. "That will probably be Jenna's department."

"Okay, because that's important too," Mom said, picking up her phone and scrolling through her messages.

"Don't worry," I said. "Our egg baby will be very well rounded."

"More like well ovaled, don't you think?" Mom guffawed at her own joke. "Get it?"

"Yes, Mom," I said, rolling my eyes. "I know egg-zactly what you mean."

CHAPTER 32

At school on Monday, Will was full of stories about Linda McMuffin's weekend. "On Friday we went to see a performance of *Phantom of the Opera* at the community theater in Greenville. She liked the music, but I think the plot was a bit too scary for her. Luckily, she still slept through the night.

"Saturday we went to the playground, and I debated letting her go down the slide, but I decided she's probably still too young."

"You think?" Jenna said, her voice oozing sarcasm. I had to agree with her.

"Will, you can *not* put an egg on a sliding board," I said. "No matter how old she is."

"I told you I didn't! But it's hard; I just want her to have fun."

Jenna shot me a look. One thing we had in common:

neither of us was sure if Linda McMuffin was going to survive having Will as a parent. His imagination might be good for school plays, but it could very well end up scrambling our egg baby.

Will took the egg baby journal out of his backpack and handed it to Jenna. "Here, you can read the rest later. I took some pictures of her too."

Jenna flipped through the journal as I looked over her shoulder. There was a picture of Linda McMuffin resting on top of a pumpkin in a pumpkin patch. Will was sitting on the ground beside her, a huge smile on his face.

"You took her pumpkin picking?" Jenna asked.

"I know, I know. I tried telling her it was a bit early in the year for that; the selection wasn't great." Will explained this as though it was the timing that was the ridiculous thing about taking an egg to visit a pumpkin patch. "But she had her heart set on pumpkins, and who can say no to that face?" He looked adoringly at Linda and stroked the top of her shell.

Jenna paused and gave Will a long look before saying, "Alrighty then! It's my turn to take her tonight." She reached out to lift Linda from Will's hands, but he pulled her back toward his chest.

"Whoa, whoa, whoa! We haven't even discussed her routine! You need to know her favorite foods and lullabies!

And she has a special blanket she sleeps with . . . wait; it's in my backpack!"

Jenna shot me a look again, then looked back at Will.

"Can I hold the egg while you look for the blanket?" she asked.

"Linda. Her name is Linda."

"I know her name is Linda. She was named after *my* grandmother, remember?"

"*Our* grandmother," I corrected her.

"Right. Our grandmother. Will, Linda belongs to all of us. You have to trust us here."

Will didn't look so sure, but he knew he didn't really have a choice. He slowly handed Linda to Jenna in a special purple fleece bag. ("I made this baby carrier for her," he explained.) Then he pulled her blanket, a small piece of green plush cloth, out of his backpack. I was impressed that Jenna didn't roll her eyes as she took it.

"Read the journal too!" Will said as Jenna took Linda over to her desk. "I wrote down lots of important information about her digestive trends!"

Jenna carefully placed Linda's box on her desk, then whispered, "You look tired. I'm going to let you get some rest tonight."

I hoped that didn't mean Jenna was going to put Linda in a corner somewhere and forget about her. I leaned forward and said, "Don't let her get *too* much rest. Remember that we have to keep a log of all her activities in a journal."

Jenna turned around. "Elfie, she's an *egg*. Even if she were a real baby, all she would do is eat, sleep, pee, and poop."

"Okay, but you still have to write that stuff down."

"I will, Elfie. Relax." Jenna started to face forward again, then turned back to me.

"Hey, my dad told me about Rhoda. Is she gonna be okay?"

I didn't know what to say. For starters, I didn't want to talk to Jenna about Rhoda, especially not right out in the open at school. It felt like something that should be kept much more private. Why did Uncle Rex have to tell her at all?

But I also simply didn't know the answer. *Was* Rhoda going to be okay? How was I supposed to know? I had asked Mom and Dad about it again the night before. Even her doctors weren't sure. She had only had a few chemotherapy sessions, and it would be months—and lots of tests—before they knew if it was working.

So I shrugged. It seemed like Jenna wanted to say more, but Ms. Rambutan asked us to take out pencils for our science test. It was a relief to start working on something with questions I knew how to answer.

CHAPTER 33

I was in my room working on the extra-credit math packet that afternoon when the phone rang. Mom answered it.

"It's Jenna," she called up the stairs. "She wants to talk to you."

Well, this was something new.

"Hi, Jenna," I said, wondering what was so important that she would call me.

"When are you going to get a phone? I hate calling people. I wish I could text you."

"Nice to speak to you too. And when would you ever text me?"

"Right now. I would text you now, for example, to ask if you can come over and help me with Linda McMuffin."

"Help you. With an egg baby." Surely I wasn't hearing her correctly.

"Yes. I don't know what to do with her. I think she's bored."

Jenna must be losing it.

"Jenna. She's an *egg*."

"I know, I know . . . but Will wrote all this fun stuff in her journal over the weekend, and I can't think of anything to say, other than the truth, which is that she's just sitting here."

"Don't you think that's probably what she did at Will's house too?"

"No! He had all those pictures of her at the playground and the pumpkin patch and the theater! You have to help me think of fun pictures to take with her too!"

"Since when do you care so much about school projects? And can't I just help you make stuff up over the phone?"

Jenna ignored my first question. "I told you, I hate talking on the phone. And I need somebody to help me stage the pictures. No one else is home right now."

"I thought you had soccer today. Just take her picture at the soccer court."

"It's a soccer *field*, not a court. But soccer was canceled; my coach is sick. I told Dad I could stay home by myself, but I need help with this."

"I don't know. I'm working on the extra-credit math packet."

"So bring it with you. I'll copy your answers when we're done with the egg pictures."

"*Jenna.*"

"I'm kidding, I'm kidding. Relax," she said. "I never do the extra-credit packets anyway!"

That was true. I wasn't sure how to answer. I really didn't feel like going to Jenna's house. But she was showing genuine interest in a school project for once . . . and she was actually asking for *my* help.

"Okay," I said. "I just have to ask my mom. But will you listen to my ideas and not boss me around?"

"Will *you* listen to *my* ideas and not boss *me* around?" she echoed back.

"I'll do my best."

"Then so will I. Now come on, get over here!"

Before I could finish saying "Let me ask my mom," Jenna had hung up. Sigh.

I put the math packet in my backpack and went downstairs.

"Mom? I need to ask you something."

Mom looked up from her laptop. "That's funny; I need to ask you something too. I just got a text from Sierra's mom. Sierra wants to know if you'd like to go to her house and see her new microscope."

"Now?"

"Yes, now. She just got it, and her mom says you were the first friend she asked to show it to. Isn't that nice?"

It was nice. It was *really* nice. It was possibly the nicest invitation I'd ever had.

"Did Sierra's mom actually use the word *friend* about me?"

Mom smiled. "Yes, she actually did."

"Is it okay if I go?"

"Of course! Let me just finish this email to a client and I'll take you over."

I started to put on my sneakers.

"Oh, Elf? What did you want to ask me?"

"Oh, right . . . um, I was wondering if you'd seen my water bottle."

Mom pointed to where the bottle sat on the kitchen counter, about two feet from me, and shook her head.

• • •

Several thoughts were swimming in my head on the way to Sierra's house:

1. Jenna didn't *really* need my help with Linda McMuffin, did she?
2. Sierra's mom said I was Sierra's friend. That must mean that Sierra had called me that too.
3. I had a friend.
4. I was actually invited over to my friend's house to hang out with her and do something fun. *My friend's* house.

5. Jenna would be fine, right? I mean, what was so hard about taking a few pictures of an egg?

6. I had lied to Mom. If I wasn't doing something wrong, why did I lie? It was just because Mom wouldn't understand; that was all it was.

7. I wished I had a phone so I could just text Jenna that I couldn't come after all, without risking Mom overhearing me.

8. I wished Jenna wasn't my cousin so I wouldn't have to worry about Mom knowing every little thing that happened between us.

• • •

As we pulled into Sierra's long gravel driveway, Mom said, "Okay, Ms. Nichols says she'll bring you home around five-thirty. Oh, and I almost forgot . . . what was Jenna calling about before?"

Uh-oh.

"Oh, I almost forgot too. She wanted to know when we could work on our egg project together."

"Oh, okay. That's nice. Good to see you two getting along."

I felt a pang in my belly.

"Yeah. Actually, could you call Jenna for me? And let her know I can't help her with the egg today? But maybe we'll do it another day?"

"Of course," Mom said, beaming. "You have a very busy social calendar this week!"

She watched me walk up the steps and waited to drive away until Sierra opened the door to let me in. As Mom gave Sierra a huge wave and a big goofy smile, I wondered which one of us was happier that I'd made a friend.

If only I could shake the nagging, Jenna-shaped ache in my stomach.

CHAPTER 34

When I got home, Dad was in the kitchen, listening to his favorite jazz station and whisking something in a bowl. Mom was leaning into the front closet, tossing out shoes.

"Didn't I ask you to put your summer sandals in your bedroom closet? You never wear them now that the weather is getting colder. In fact, they probably won't even fit you next year. Just put them in the donation bag in the laundry room. And I don't want to hear anything about the cave crickets. Be brave!"

Urft. Mom was in some kind of mood. All I'd done was walk through the door, and I already felt like I was in trouble for something.

"Okay," I said. "Is everything all right?"

"Everything is fine." Mom's tight voice sounded anything but fine.

Dad gave me a small smile and a wave from the kitchen. "Hi, honey. Did you have fun at Sierra's?"

"Yes." I'd been excited to tell Mom and Dad everything about my time at Sierra's house . . . how her microscope was amazing, and we looked at chicken feathers and goat fur through it and made her brothers guess which was which. And that Sierra likes baking too, so we made brownies from a mix, but she said next time she'd ask her mom to get more ingredients and maybe we could make doughnuts or cake pops. And that her favorite show is also *Superstars of Science.*

But Mom's mood was catching (just like her laugh, Mom's bad moods could be contagious), and suddenly I didn't feel like talking about any of that.

"How are you guys?"

"Well, I had an interesting afternoon," Mom said, still in her tight voice. "I met my egg grandchild, Linda McMuffin. She's very cute. I'm just sorry you weren't there for the occasion."

"You met Linda McMuffin? Did Jenna come here?"

"No, she did not. I went to their house."

"Oh. I didn't know you were planning to go over there."

"I wasn't. But when I called Jenna to tell her you went to Sierra's house and that you'd work on your project another day, she started crying."

"*Crying?* Are you sure? Jenna doesn't cry. At least not about school stuff."

"Yes, she does cry, Elfie. Everyone cries. And she wasn't crying about school; she was crying because you let her down. And because she was home by herself and feeling miserable. Why didn't you tell me that you'd promised to go there today?"

"I didn't promise! I mean . . . I said I would, but I wasn't sure; I hadn't even asked you yet."

"And what do you think I would have said?"

I didn't answer. Of course she would have said yes.

"Elfie, I know you and Jenna have never really hit it off. But . . ."

"I know, I know," I said. "But she's family, and I have to try harder."

"That's not what I was going to say," Mom said. "Although that is true. But what I was going to say is that Jenna's going through a really tough time. I don't think she needed help with the school project today as much as she just needed someone to be with her. And she wanted that someone to be you, Elf."

"I'm sure I wasn't her first choice. Esme and five other people were probably busy."

"That's not the point. She thought you were coming over and you basically stood her up. I wound up going there to help with her pictures."

"Okay, but did she really even need help with the pictures? Jenna takes pictures with her phone all the time. She seems to be pretty skilled at it."

"Also not the point, Elfie. I told you, I think she just didn't want to be alone."

How was this happening? How was it possible that Mom was mad at me for not dropping everything and going to Jenna's house when Jenna had been shirking group projects and hanging out with her other friends and doing her own thing for years?

"I'm sorry if I wanted to hang out with my friend instead!" I yelled, in a way that said I wasn't actually sorry at all. "I'm sorry if I wanted to let Jenna work on a project by herself for a change so I could go to a friend's house! I finally get to do something fun, and now Jenna's getting me in trouble for it!"

I grabbed my backpack, ran upstairs, and slammed my bedroom door. I didn't even feel like working on the math extra credit anymore; that's how mad I was. I needed Rhoda. She would have understood. I wanted to email her, but the computer was downstairs, and I didn't want to be anywhere near Mom just then. So I did what I used to do when I needed to tell Rhoda something.

I took the Important Jar off its shelf and wiped a thin layer of dust off the lid. It had never gotten dusty before, because it had never gone this long without someone using it. I tore up a piece of paper and put three notes inside the jar:

- I miss you.
- I made a new friend.
- Mom likes Jenna more than she likes me.

I didn't know when I would see Rhoda again, but somehow writing the notes to her still made me feel a little bit better.

• • •

Mom knocked on my door about half an hour later.

"Dinner's almost ready."

"I'm not hungry."

"It's French toast." Mom knew how much I loved breakfast foods for dinner. But I stayed quiet. I heard Mom sigh on the other side of the door.

"Can I come in, Elf? I feel like we should talk."

I opened my door and let her in. But I still didn't say anything.

"I thought about what you said," Mom said, sitting beside me on my bed, "and I think you're right."

"You do?" I hadn't expected her to say that.

"Yes, about some of it. It makes sense that you wanted to go to Sierra's house; I know you're excited about your new friendship with her."

I waited for Mom to continue. I knew there was a *but* coming.

"But"—there it was—"do you think that was the best way for you to handle it? To tell Jenna you'd come over, and then just not show up? You should have told me. I could have helped you sort it out."

"I thought if I told you, then you'd make me go to Jenna's."

Mom shook her head. "I don't think so. It's important for you to have a friend like Sierra. We could have figured out another time to go to Jenna's. But it would have been nice to at least tell her first."

I looked down at my bedspread and nodded.

Mom sighed again. "I'm sorry I got so worked up about this. But I worry about Jenna sometimes. I know you think she has it all figured out, but divorce can really be horrendous. When Grandma and Grandpa got divorced when I was a kid, at least Uncle Rex and I had each other to lean on. Jenna's having to weather this as an only child."

"I know," I said. "Poor only children. They are so super lonely and weird. Why would their terrible parents ever do that to them?"

Mom caught my small smile. "Oh, are we joking instead of yelling now?" she said, reaching out and messing up my hair. As she brought her hand back, she glanced to the side and saw the Important Jar sitting on my bedside table.

"Oh, your Important Jar," she said.

I remembered the note I'd just written about her liking Jenna more than she liked me. It didn't seem fair now.

"Don't open it!" I said.

"I won't, hon; I know these notes are between you and Rhoda. But . . ."

"I know, I know; we don't even know when we're going to see Rhoda again. It just makes me feel better to write to her, that's all."

"I hear you," Mom said. "Actually, I wanted to ask you about that. . . . How would you like to see Rhoda tomorrow?"

"Tomorrow? Really?"

"Yep. I talked to Betty today, and she's not able to stay with Rhoda during her chemo treatment tomorrow, so she wanted to know if we could go instead. Do you think you're up for that?"

"Yes! I told you I could handle it."

"Okay, then we're on. I'm going down to see if Dad needs help with dinner; can you join us in five minutes for some French toast?"

"Yes, definitely." I watched Mom go, then opened the Important Jar, took out the note about her liking Jenna more, and threw it away.

CHAPTER 35

"That's all Linda did at your house? Read books with your aunt?" Will was clearly disappointed in Jenna's pictures of Linda's activities from the night before. He took a bite of his sandwich as he flipped through the pages of the egg baby journal. We were in the cafeteria, eating lunch. The ant population had dwindled, which Will had warned us would probably happen as the weather got cooler. But he, Maxine, and I still sat together. Will and Maxine talked a lot about what they planned to sing for the school musical auditions, and whether Will should dye all of his hair purple or just the front. I didn't talk much about myself, but that was okay. I didn't really feel like talking to Will and Maxine about the things that were on my mind anyway—namely Hampshire Academy and Rhoda.

Today Jenna was with us too, since there was new egg baby information to discuss. She sounded hurt by Will's tone as he looked at her pictures of Linda. "What's wrong with reading books? It was a school night. I also made her some little hats."

Will squinted at the brightly colored bits of cloth on Linda's head in each picture. "Those are *hats*?" he said. "I thought it was just weird fuzz coming off Elfie's mom's sweater. You should see Maxine's egg; she has all these different springy antenna headbands."

"I know," Jenna said quietly. "Esme showed me."

I felt like I had to defend Jenna, especially after all that Mom had told me about how she was feeling yesterday. "Those are obviously hats," I said. "And reading with Linda is a good thing. Literacy is very important, even for babies. And they should hear thirty thousand words per day for optimal speech development."

"She probably heard that many words in ten minutes when she was with Will," Jenna muttered.

Will didn't take Jenna's bait. "Yes, easily!" he agreed. "Okay, well, I was just concerned that her evening wasn't very interesting. But if Elfie thinks this was a good idea, then I guess I'll allow it."

Jenna leaned forward; I noticed her hands were clenched into fists at her sides. "You'll *allow* it?" she said. "You're not her only parent, you know! And why is it okay if Elfie says it is, but not me?"

"It's nothing personal," Will said. "Elfie's just always been really good in school, so I value her opinion on these things."

"I see." Jenna's fists looked even tighter. "How could I possibly take that personally." She picked up her lunch tray and carried it over to Esme's table.

"You hurt her feelings," I said.

"How?" Will seemed genuinely surprised. "It's true; you're really smart."

I felt my cheeks get warm. This was an odd sensation: feeling bad for Jenna at the same time I felt flattered by a compliment from a classmate. Both were new experiences for me.

"Well. Thank you. But Jenna should know we care about what she thinks too."

"Do we?" Will said. I couldn't tell if he was joking or not.

"Yes, we do. Or at least we should. She's in our group too." Wow, Mom would be ridiculously proud of me right now.

Will thought for a second. "Okay. Should we let her have an extra night? I mean, I got to have Linda over the weekend, and Jenna just had her one night. The journal isn't due until next week."

"Okay," I said. "But let me tell her. I have to talk to her anyway."

I stood at Jenna and Esme's table for a full five seconds before Jenna looked up at me. "What?" She said it in an annoyed way, like I was interrupting something important. Esme didn't look at me at all.

"Can I talk to you? Alone?"

"Why can't we talk here?"

I thought for a second. "It's about the egg baby project, and I don't want any other groups to hear our ideas."

Esme did look up at me then, and rolled her eyes. "Don't worry, Elfie; I'm sure you'll still get the very highest grade in the class."

"Thank you, Esme," I said. "I'm sure you're right."

Jenna groaned, but she got up and followed me to the corner by the recycling bin. "You're so weird, Elfie. What do you need to say?"

I took a deep breath. "Well, first I want to say I'm sorry. I know I"—what was the term Mom had used?—"*stood you up* yesterday so I could go to my friend Sierra's house. And I shouldn't have done it."

"You're just saying that because your mom made you."

"No, I'm not. My mom's not here right now; how would she even know I'm apologizing?"

"She could ask me later."

I sighed. "Can't you just trust me? I really am sorry. And I stuck up for you with Will, about the pictures of Mom reading with Linda."

Jenna looked down and twisted her friendship bracelets. "I know. Thanks for that."

"You're welcome."

"Okay. Is that all?"

"No, that's not all. Will and I think you should get to have an extra night with Linda, since he had the whole weekend. So you can take her home if you want. But I actually have another idea of something we could do."

"What?"

"Do you think Linda McMuffin would be interested in visiting a hospital?"

CHAPTER 36

I'm not sure why I decided to invite Jenna to come with us to visit Rhoda. If someone had asked me a week ago to name people I would want to accompany me to visit Rhoda during one of her chemotherapy treatments, Jenna wouldn't have even been on the list. No way. But I was still thinking about how Mom said Jenna had cried, and I couldn't shake it out of my head. Besides, if I went to Jenna's house to help with Linda today, then I wouldn't be able to visit Rhoda. This way, I could do both.

Jenna held Linda on the way to the hospital. She was in the special baby carrier Will had made for her.

"Will is really into this egg baby project, isn't he?" Jenna said as she nestled the baby carrier into the back seat beside her.

"He truly is. I think it's replaced the cafeteria ants as his favorite thing."

Jenna laughed. "What did you say they're called? Sidewalk ants?"

"No, pavement ants. That's their common name. The scientific name is *Tetramorium caespitum*."

"Right," Jenna said. "I don't know how you remember stuff like that."

She was quiet for a second as she looked out the car window. "Hey, do you know what's going on with that other school? Hampshire? Are they going to let you back in? Talking about the scientific ant name made me think of it again."

I saw Mom glance at me out of the corner of her eye. She knew this was not my favorite subject to discuss, especially not with Jenna. But Jenna seemed genuinely curious; for once I didn't mind talking about it with her.

"I don't really know," I said. "My friend Sierra told them her side of the story—which is the same as *my* side of the story, that I didn't do anything wrong—but the honor code review board hasn't met yet. They just told her they'd 'take what she said into consideration.'"

"It's hard to be patient," Mom said.

Jenna nodded. "Yeah. Waiting is the worst."

"Well, one wait is almost over," Mom said as she switched on the left-turn signal to go into the hospital parking lot. "You finally get to see Rhoda."

• • •

The first thing Mom, Jenna, and I passed after walking through the big front doors of the hospital was a hand sanitizer dispenser, and we all used it. The second thing we passed was a gift shop.

"Do you think we should get something for Rhoda here?" Jenna asked. "Maybe some candy?"

I shook my head. "Rhoda emailed me the other day that her chemotherapy treatments usually make her feel nauseous. So she tries to just eat something really boring (usually toast or rice) on her chemo days. She said if she eats something she loves, like chocolate, she might develop an aversion to it and never want to eat it again."

Jenna pursed her lips and nodded. "Okay," she said in a small voice. I couldn't remember the last time she'd been so quietly accepting of one of my explanations. I think the hospital was making her a little scared. I felt the same way, but I didn't want to show it.

"Besides, *we're* her present. Just us visiting is going to cheer her up. Right, Mom?" My voice didn't sound like it belonged to me.

"That's right, Elf." Mom gave my shoulder a squeeze. "And you can introduce her to Linda. She'll get a kick out of that."

We took the elevator to the eighth floor and followed the "Oncology Outpatient Unit" signs, just as Betty had instructed us to do. We walked through what felt like a giant maze and finally wound up at a desk at the end of a long hallway. A lady behind the desk asked if she could help us, and Mom said we were there to visit Rhoda.

The lady smiled. "Oh, she told me she was excited for her visitors today. If you could just sign in and take a minute to wash your hands, I'll point you in the right direction."

Mom wrote our names on a clipboard, then she, Jenna, and I washed our hands at a sink in the hallway beside the desk. A sign above the sink said:

Chemotherapy Patients Are at Increased Risk of Infection
SANITIZE HANDS HERE

It was a lot of serious words in a small space. I suddenly felt even more nervous than I already had.

After we dried our hands on paper towels, the lady behind the desk directed us to walk down a long corridor lined with big white reclining chairs separated by flowered curtains. Each recliner had two smaller chairs beside it. Most of the recliners had people sitting in them, with tubes going into their arms from machines. Some, but not all, of the people in recliners had guests with them.

I tried not to stare at the people in the recliners, but it was hard. For one thing, it wasn't something I was used to seeing: a long row of people hooked up to machines. Some of the people were completely bald. Others were wearing hats or scarves, but if you looked closely, you could see that they were bald underneath. A few had hair; I wondered if they were wearing wigs. It was a lot to take in.

But I also felt like I almost had to stare in order to figure out which of the people was *my* person. My Rhoda. Usually I could spot her from far away with her long, dark wavy hair, but of course that was gone now.

Mom must have been thinking the same thing, because she also had stopped at the end of the corridor and was trying to casually scan the row of patients. But then we heard a familiar voice.

"Justine! Jenna! Ellllfie! Down here!"

At the very end of the corridor, one patient was leaning forward and giving us a little wave. She was wearing jeans, an orange sweater, and a bright blue head scarf covered in butterflies. Rhoda.

Mom zipped down and grasped both of Rhoda's hands in hers. "Hey there, kid!" she said. Jenna and I followed, but I wasn't sure what to do. Part of me wanted to hug Rhoda, but another part of me was afraid. Was I even allowed to hug her? What if a hug knocked out her tubes?

Rhoda grabbed my hands next. She looked really different. Even though she had the scarf on, it was easy to tell she was bald underneath. Something else was different too, but it took me a moment to figure out what it was. Her eyebrows. They were gone. It hadn't occurred to me that the chemotherapy would also make her eyebrows fall out. But her eyes had a smile in them the way they always did. Her eyes were the same.

"Hey, it's okay," she said, looking up at me. "I'm still me, remember? You reminded me about that, in your email."

"I know," I said, making a small laughing sound as if to show that I didn't need reassurance. But Rhoda knew me better than that.

She gave my hands a squeeze and reached for Jenna's next. "And Jenna too! How'd I get so lucky to have so many cool kids visit me?"

"You're sure it's not too much?" Mom said. She had texted with both Rhoda and Betty earlier to make sure it was okay to have three visitors, and they had both said she would love it. Rhoda repeated that now.

"Are you kidding?" she said. "This feels like a party!"

"Okay," Mom said, "but I think we'll still go in shifts. Jenna, do you want to see what kind of ice cream the cafeteria has?"

Mom knew I'd want some time alone with Rhoda, and Jenna seemed to get it too. She gamely followed Mom back to the elevator, and I sat down in one of Rhoda's visitor chairs.

"So." Rhoda looked up at the machine pumping medicine into her arm, then back at me. "Is it super weird to see me like this? I mean, I know I almost never wear orange." She pointed both index fingers toward her orange sweater.

I laughed. Only Rhoda would know how to make me laugh at a time like this. "Yes, the sweater is extremely weird," I said.

Rhoda smiled. "I know it's got to seem strange. It's still pretty strange for me, and I've been doing this for a little while now."

"How do you feel?" I asked. "Does it hurt?"

She shook her head. "Nah, not in the way you'd think. I mean, there's a sharp prick for a second when they put the needle in your arm, but I've gotten used to feeling like a pincushion. The hard part about it is that it makes me feel really, really tired for a day or two. And most days it also makes me feel really sick; I've thrown up a few times."

"*Urft,*" I said.

"Yeah. *Urft.* But it's better to be getting sick from the medicine than from the cancer."

"That's true." I wasn't sure what was the best way to ask my next question, so I just blurted it out. "Is the medicine working?"

"It's too soon to tell. The doctors will do some tests at the end of this round of chemo and see what they can find out. That will tell them if they have to do more. So for now we just have to wait."

"Waiting is the worst." I thought of how Jenna had just said that in the car, about me waiting to hear news about Hampshire. But waiting to hear news about Rhoda's health was much, much harder.

"Yeah, I hate it too."

Rhoda reached out and rubbed the soft fleece of Linda McMuffin's baby carrier. "What's in here?" she asked.

I suddenly felt silly telling Rhoda about Linda McMuffin, and I certainly didn't want to take pictures of Linda here; what was I thinking? Did Rhoda even want to be in pictures these days, looking as different as she did from her usual self?

But as I was trying to come up with an answer, Rhoda got distracted by something behind me.

"Hey there, lady! I wondered if you were coming today!"

I turned and saw a woman with blue eyes settling into the space beside Rhoda's. Like Rhoda, she seemed to be bald, but instead of a scarf, she was wearing a pink baseball cap with little tennis rackets embroidered on the brim. And she was older than Rhoda, closer to Mom's age.

"Hey, Rhoda," the lady said, putting her purse down and sitting in the recliner. "The traffic was terrible, plus my mother drives like an old lady. I suppose that's because she *is* an old lady."

Rhoda laughed. "I know how that goes. April, this is Elfie, who I've told you so much about. Elfie, this is April, my favorite chemo-mate."

"It's nice to meet you, Elfie." April smiled. "Oh, Rhoda, I brought that book I mentioned the other day. It's in my other bag; my son's bringing it up. He was going to stop by the snack machine first."

"Ooh!" Rhoda sounded excited. "Do I finally get to meet your son today?"

April smiled. "Yes, we forced him to come. He has lacrosse practice after this, and my mom told him if he wanted a ride, he'd have to tag along because she won't drive all over creation for him. She doesn't mess around."

Yesterday I might have been surprised that a kid wouldn't want to be with his mom during her chemo appointment. I'd been asking Mom forever if we could see Rhoda here. But now I could understand why it might not be too easy. Even when the patients seemed cheerful, like Rhoda and April, there was still a sadness in this place.

Rhoda leaned forward and gave a wave. From where I was sitting behind the curtain, I couldn't see who she was waving at; I assumed it was Mom and Jenna, returning from the cafeteria.

But I was wrong.

"This must be them," Rhoda said.

April leaned forward and looked down the corridor. "Yes, that's my entourage," she said with a laugh.

I turned to see an old lady with a big purse walking briskly toward us. Like April, she was petite and blue eyed; her hair was short and white. Then I saw the boy, April's son, walking slowly behind her.

He was carrying a large canvas bag with "April" stitched onto the side. He was a bit taller than me, with light brown hair that flopped in front of his eyes. He was frowning. He was someone I knew, someone I hadn't seen in a while. He was the last person I expected to see in the hospital that day.

He was Colton Palmer.

CHAPTER 37

It felt like the air had gone out of the room. I didn't know what to do. I'd thought about Colton and what he did every day. Even though I'd only met him once, he had become something like a monster in my mind. And here he was, right on the other side of a thin curtain. Visiting his mom, who was having her chemotherapy treatment.

I was trapped. I turned my back to the curtain and tried to make myself as small as I could. I pulled my knees up to my chest and wrapped my arms around them.

"Are you okay?" Rhoda asked. "I know it gets cold in here; do you want to use my coat as a blanket?"

I shook my head. "No, it's okay." I did not want to use Rhoda's coat as a blanket. I did not want to be there at all anymore. I wanted to escape.

April's voice drifted over from her recliner. "Rhoda, this is my mom and my son, Cole." (*Cole?*) "Guys, this is my friend Rhoda."

The old lady—Colton's grandma—gave Rhoda a small nod. "Pleasure meeting you." If Colton said anything, I didn't hear it. But it's possible that my hearing was compromised because I had half buried my face in my arms.

"It's nice to meet you too," Rhoda said. "I've heard so much about you both. This is Elfie."

Without picking my head up off my knees, I gave a quick little wave with my right hand. Rhoda gave me a wide-eyed look that said, *What's the matter with you?* I could tell I was embarrassing her by being so unfriendly, but what else could I do?

Then there were new voices in the corridor. Mom and Jenna.

"Okay," Jenna was announcing as she came nearer. "The cafeteria only has vanilla and mint chocolate chip today, but they also have brownies if anyone wants one." She stopped as she reached our nook, and her face turned pink.

"Oh man, Rhoda, I'm sorry . . . I forgot about your eating rules." Jenna's face went from pink to red. I'd never seen her this uncomfortable.

"It's okay, Jenna; I know it's hard to imagine me not wanting sweets!" Rhoda smiled at her. "Hey, I want you guys to meet my friend April and her family."

As the introductions were being made, Colton's mom again called him Cole, so I knew Mom wouldn't make the connection. I felt like my scalp was on fire. How could this be happening? It didn't seem real.

"Hey," Jenna said, walking over to my chair, "did you tell Rhoda about Linda yet?"

"Yes, I already did," I said quickly. "I emailed her about it."

"Oh, okay . . . but has she seen her?"

"Wait . . . you brought Linda McMuffin with you today?" Rhoda sounded genuinely excited. "How could you not have told me yet? I want to meet her!"

"Who's Linda McMuffin?" April asked.

"She's our egg baby," Jenna said. "It's a project we're doing for school."

From behind the curtain, I heard Colton laugh. "An *egg* baby?"

"Cole," his mother said in a warning tone.

"Sorry," he said. "It just sounded funny to me, an egg baby for a school assignment."

I couldn't take it. Not only had this kid cheated, lied, and gotten me kicked out of Hampshire Academy, but now he was laughing at Linda McMuffin, our egg project, and, by extension, Ms. Rambutan and Cottonwood Elementary. It bothered me. A lot.

I sprang out of my chair and turned to face him. "So I

guess you wouldn't do something so dumb at your school, huh? You know what else we do at my school that you don't do at yours? We tell the truth. And treat each other fairly."

It was hard to say who looked most shocked: Colton, Jenna, or any of the staring grown-ups. Mom was the only one who could find her voice.

"*Elfie!* What's going on?"

But I was still looking at Colton. "I don't know if you remember me. I went to your school for about five minutes. But thanks to you, I got kicked out for something I didn't do. And your mom might call you Cole, but that day you said your name was Colton. Maybe that's another lie you were telling."

I heard Mom make a little gasping sound. I wanted to turn and run down the corridor, but something made my feet stay.

"Why did you do that, by the way?" I asked. "Why did you let the headmaster believe I stole your phone? Why did you lie?"

Colton looked at the floor. "You did take my phone," he mumbled.

"You know what I mean," I said. "You know what really happened."

"What's this all about, Cole?" Colton's mom seemed genuinely perplexed.

"Elfie." Mom's voice was quiet. "Maybe you and Colton can talk later. But not here."

Tears had started running down my cheeks; I wiped them on my sleeve, and I suddenly felt horrid. I knew Mom was right. I couldn't believe I was yelling in this place, at this time, in front of Rhoda and Colton's mom as they had tubes pumping chemicals into their bodies. I thought I might be sick.

"I'm sorry, Rhoda," I sniffed. "I'm so sorry. I'll email you later; I promise."

I thrust Linda McMuffin's baby carrier into Jenna's hands, grabbed my jacket, and ran down the corridor to the elevator.

CHAPTER 38

Just as the elevator doors were about to close, an arm covered in friendship bracelets was quickly thrust in between them, and the doors bounced back open. Jenna.

But she wasn't alone. She hopped onto the elevator, and Colton quickly stepped in behind her.

"Why are *you* here?" I glared at him, then looked to Jenna as the elevator doors closed. She shrugged and grimaced.

"I told my mom I had to talk to you," Colton said. "My grandma said she would explain the rest."

"She'll probably just tell your mom all the same lies you've been telling all along."

Colton shook his head. "Nah, probably not. I'm guessing my grandma's on your side here."

I snorted. "I seriously doubt that."

Colton sighed. "No, it's true. Sierra Nichols wrote an email to the honor review board and told them what happened. My whole family knows about it now. Except for my mom. We're not supposed to tell her anything that might upset her these days."

"She seems like she could handle it," I said.

He laughed. "Yeah, that's the ironic part. She's probably stronger than all the rest of them put together."

"Hey, good example of irony!" Jenna said. Maybe she paid more attention in school than I thought.

"Thanks?" Colton said, giving Jenna a strange look.

The elevator had reached the ground floor; we stepped out into the hospital lobby.

"Anyway, look," Colton said, "I'm sorry about everything that happened."

"What in particular?" I asked. "Making fun of us and our school just now? Trying to cheat on the marshmallow project? Or accusing me of stealing and getting me kicked out of school?"

"*That's* what happened?" Jenna gasped. "*This kid* got you kicked out? Also, what's a marshmallow project?"

"I'll tell you later. But yeah, that's what happened."

Jenna inhaled sharply. "My dad told me a little about it, but not the whole story. You would never steal anything!" She turned to Colton and repeated herself. "Elfie would never steal anything."

"I know," Colton said. "She grabbed my phone because I was about to use it for a project and we weren't supposed to."

"Oh yeah, *that* sounds like something Elfie would do." Jenna looked at me and nodded.

"But he let the headmaster believe I stole it, and then they kicked me out."

"Yeah, that's the part I'm most sorry about. I never actually thought they'd suspend you."

"Why, though?" By then I felt almost more confused than angry. "Why did you let it happen?"

"I guess I couldn't see a way out. If I told them the truth, then they'd know what I was trying to do. I didn't want to get in trouble and stress my family out more than they already are. There's just been a lot going on with us."

"I know how that goes," I pointed out. "There's been a lot going on with us too."

Colton nodded. "Yeah, I can see that. Anyway, I'll talk to them. I'm going to tell them you and Sierra were telling the truth."

Was he serious? He was really going to tell the honor review board the truth? Did that mean they would say I could go back to Hampshire? Before I could think of how to respond, the elevator doors opened again, and Colton's grandma stepped out.

"There you are," she said, then looked at Jenna and me. "Is everything all right down here?"

"Yes," I said. "We're okay." To my surprise, it felt like the truth.

"Good, good." Colton's grandma nodded and looked at him. "You need to come back up and see your mother."

Colton looked pale.

"Come on," his grandma said. "She's actually taking it pretty well. This is not the way I would have suggested telling her this news, but she and Mrs. Oster have been talking, and so far, so good." I felt my cheeks get warm as I imagined the conversation happening upstairs.

Colton's grandma looked at me as she pressed the elevator button. "Your mother says she's leaving soon; I'll let her know you're down here."

"Thank you," I said.

Colton raised his hand slightly from where it hung by his waist. "See you later," he said.

"See you later," I repeated, but I wondered if I really would.

· · ·

"Wow. You really gave it to that kid," Jenna said after the elevator doors closed. "I'm impressed." She pointed to her right, down the hallway. "The cafeteria's that way. Want to get some ice cream now? I think Linda wants some too." She held the egg baby carrier up, as though to show me Linda looking hungry.

I suddenly felt weak. "I feel terrible about the way I ran out of there; Rhoda must be so upset."

"I wouldn't worry; if anyone understands, it's Rhoda." Jenna pulled her phone out of her back pocket. "Here, I'll text your mom and tell her where we are; do you want to say anything else?"

"Can you just ask her to tell Rhoda I'm sorry and I feel awful?"

Jenna tapped at her phone screen for a minute.

"Done. Now can we please get some ice cream? My treat."

"Okay," I said. I wasn't used to Jenna being so nice to me; I felt like I should acknowledge it somehow. "And thank you. This is, um, very nice of you."

"I know, I know," she said, patting me on the back as we walked toward the cafeteria. "This is you being effusive."

• • •

Jenna and I were almost finished with our ice cream when Mom joined us in the cafeteria.

"How's it going down here?" she asked.

"It's fine," I said. "Please go ahead and say whatever you're going to say to me." I wanted to hear what kind of trouble I was in and get it over with.

Mom sighed. "I don't know what to say, Elf. That was a tough scene."

"I'm sorry; I was just really shocked, and—"

"No, I don't think you need to apologize." Mom shook

her head. "Colton—or Cole, or whatever his name is—really put you through the mill, and you didn't expect to see him here, of all places."

"Oh. You're not mad at me for yelling at him?"

"Like you said, Elf, you were shocked. We all were."

"Is Rhoda mad at me?"

"You know it would take a lot more than that to make Rhoda mad at you. She understands. She might have felt awkward, but she definitely understands. Her mom is coming to pick her up soon, and she said she'll call you when she gets home."

"What happened after we left?" Jenna asked.

"Colton's grandma told his mom what happened on the first day of school. They'd been keeping it from her since she's been sick."

"Did you tell him Elfie's side?"

"I filled in a few details here and there when they asked for them. But his dad and his grandma have a pretty clear picture, thanks to Sierra."

"What did his mom say?" I couldn't imagine how she felt hearing that story, sitting there in the hospital.

"She was disappointed. And extremely apologetic. I told her we were still waiting to hear the honor committee's verdict, and she said she'd talk to Colton. She's probably doing that right now. . . . I left when Colton and his grandma came back up to the chemo unit."

Mom paused. "She also said Colton's been having a very hard time with her illness. Remember Sierra's dad saying that Colton had missed a lot of school this year? I suspect that this is why. It's all a good reminder that everyone you meet has a story you don't know."

"That doesn't make what he did to Elfie okay, though," Jenna pointed out.

"That's exactly what his mother said. And she also asked if there was anything she could do to help."

"She might not need to now," I said. "Colton said he'll tell the honor review board the whole story."

Mom raised her eyebrows. "That would be amazing."

"You sound like you're not sure you believe him," Jenna said.

"No, I guess I'm not."

"Me neither." Jenna shook her head as she scraped at the sides of her ice cream cup with her wooden spoon.

"What do you think, Elf?" Mom rested her chin on her hand and looked at me.

What did I think? I had no idea. All of this suddenly felt way too big and grown-up and exhausting for me. At the moment, I only knew one thing for sure, and that was that I wanted to go home.

CHAPTER 39

"We still haven't taken any pictures of Linda McMuffin," I said, cutting my egg roll in half to let the steam escape. Dad had a late meeting at the library, and Mom had stopped to pick up Chinese food on the way home from the hospital. ("I'm much too wrung out from our afternoon to even think about cooking," she said.)

"I know," Jenna said as she tried to pick up her noodles with chopsticks. "But it would have felt weird to take pictures of her at the hospital; I didn't know how to ask about that."

"Me neither," I said. "I'm glad we didn't."

"You can at least write about her trip to the hospital in your egg baby journal, can't you?" Mom said. "And then we can take pictures of her doing something else."

"Hoo boy, I hope that's good enough for Will," Jenna said.

Mom looked surprised. "I thought Will never cared about getting good grades."

"He doesn't usually," I agreed, "but this egg baby project has brought out a whole new Will."

Jenna backed me up. "Yeah, he's a real helicopter parent for this egg. He just hovers around her all the time. I'm surprised he even agreed to let me have a second night with her."

"Well, let me know if you think of some photo opportunities, and I'd be happy to help you," Mom said. "Maybe take pictures of her with our dinner? Egg baby with egg rolls?"

"*Urft*, Mom, that was a bad joke."

"Sorry, I should have covered Linda McMuffin's ears." Mom looked around. "Where is she, anyway?"

"I put her in the living room." Jenna pointed to where Linda was resting on top of a bookshelf.

What happened then was a blur. One second Goober had been winding around Mom's ankles at the kitchen sink; the next second he was in the living room.

On top of the bookshelf.

Knocking things off with his furry little paw.

Mom and Dad's wedding picture was the first to go. It fell to the floor with a crash. It was followed by a clay pinch pot I'd made for Dad in kindergarten.

By then it was easy to see what was coming. Jenna and I moved as fast as we could, but we were too late. Just before we reached the bookshelf, Goober gave Linda McMuffin a mighty swat, and our egg baby plummeted to the floor. Her shattered shell was scattered among the broken glass and pottery, and her yolk oozed over Mom and Dad's smiling wedding-day faces.

It was like a crime scene.

"GOOBER!" Mom yelled.

"Bad kitty!" Jenna added. "Bad, *bad* kitty!"

Goober ran off, probably to hide under my bed until he thought he was out of trouble. I stared at the mess. There was no way to salvage it. The biggest piece of Linda that was still intact had one green eye and half her little smile on it. It really couldn't be any worse.

"Oh, girls," Mom said. "I'm so sorry. I feel like this is partly my fault; I'm the one who laughed at Goober every time he knocked oranges off the counter. He thought it was a game."

"No, it's my fault," Jenna said. "I should have known better than to put Linda on a shelf. I'm really sorry, Elfie."

They both looked at me like they were afraid *I* was going to break next.

"Elfie. Say something." Jenna sounded nervous.

I could only think of one thing to say. *"Urft."*

"Urft? All you have to say is *urft?* Our egg baby just bit the dust! That little thing was growing on me! Plus, we might get an F on our project now. Aren't you freaking out?"

"We're not going to get an F," I said. My voice was the calmest in the room for once. "We have good pictures, and a good journal. And now we have a new story to add.

Ms. Rambutan wanted us to learn something from this, right? Well, we *learned* that we should keep a closer eye on babies around cats. And maybe not put them on bookcases."

"I guess . . . ," Jenna said.

"Jenna, listen . . . I'm not worried. I figure we've also learned lately that there are bigger problems than broken eggs. There are even bigger problems than getting kicked out of schools like Hampshire. We can tell Ms. Rambutan that if we have to; I feel like she'd listen."

"Yeah, okay." Jenna nodded. "If you aren't worried, then neither am I."

Mom gave each of us a squeeze. "I'm proud of you girls. Go finish your homework; I'll clean up poor Miss Linda here."

"Oh, but one more thing that might *actually* be a problem . . ." The thought occurred to me as I reached into my backpack for the egg baby journal. "How are we going to explain this to Will?"

CHAPTER 40

It would be an understatement to say Will was angry.

Will was incredulous.

Will was outraged.

Will was devastated.

We knew this because he said all these things when we told him what happened to Linda. "I am incredulous. I am outraged. I am devastated. I am speechless."

"You don't seem very speechless," Jenna said.

I tried to reassure him. "I'll talk to Ms. Rambutan. I don't think this has to mean we get a bad grade."

"I don't care about the *grade*!" Will howled. "I care about Linda!"

Ms. Rambutan came over to see what was going on.

"Is everything okay in this group? Where is Linda McMuffin?"

"She is not here because she has been *murdered*!" Will was really laying it on thick.

"She wasn't *murdered*." Jenna rolled her eyes at Will. "She fell."

"Fell?" Will actually clutched at his chest. "She didn't fall. She was pushed!"

"Uh-oh." Ms. Rambutan sounded genuinely concerned. "How did that happen?"

"My cat knocked her off a shelf." Compared to breaking the news to Will, telling Ms. Rambutan wasn't so bad.

"Oh dear. Well, that'll do it."

"She must have been terrified." Will sniffled. "Elfie's cat probably looked like a tiger to her."

"I'm sorry." Ms. Rambutan grabbed a tissue from the table behind her and handed it to Will. "I know this must be hard. Once you've had time to collect your feelings a bit, you have a couple of options. You have a few days of the assignment left, so I can give you a fresh egg to continue with."

Will sniffled again. "No one could ever replace Linda." He picked up Linda's empty baby carrier from where Jenna had laid it on her desk and held it to his heart.

"Okay. *Or* you could finish the assignment now, although I should tell you that if you go that route, you will have some points deducted for being a few days short on journal entries. Either way, I'd expect you to write an account of what happened in your egg baby journal, as well as a reflection on what you've learned, of course."

"Do you guys know what you want to do?" I asked Will and Jenna. Will blew his nose and shook his head.

Jenna sighed. "I think we're going to need some more time."

"That's fine," Ms. Rambutan said. "But please let me know by the end of the day so I know whether I should bring in a fresh egg tomorrow."

"I need to be alone with my thoughts on this for a while," Will said after Ms. Rambutan walked away. "Can we reconvene after lunch?"

"Suuurre." Jenna drew the word out, like she was trying to handle Will extra carefully. She watched him walk to his desk, still holding the egg baby carrier, then turned to me.

"It sounds like he needs some space from us. You can sit with me and Esme today at lunch if you want."

I'd been less surprised when Goober sent Linda crashing to the ground.

"Oh, okay. Thanks."

I couldn't picture sitting with Jenna at lunch. And certainly not Esme. But was it even necessary? Was Will so upset that he wouldn't want me to sit with him?

. . .

Yes, apparently Will was just that upset. He and Maxine got to the cafeteria before I did, and as I approached our usual table—the ant table, we'd gotten in the habit of calling it— Will held out his hand to stop me, like a crossing guard.

"Elfie, I hope we can resolve this eventually, but I don't think it's a good idea for us to sit together today. I really do need some time alone with my thoughts."

"You aren't alone. You're with Maxine."

"I need some time alone with my thoughts *and* Maxine. She is the sounding board for my thoughts."

Maxine looked at me and mouthed, "Sorry." I retreated with my lunch box and went to Jenna and Esme's table.

Jenna slid over so I could sit beside her. I saw her give Esme a look that seemed meaningful, but I couldn't tell why. Did it mean *I'm sorry* or *Be nice*? Or something else altogether?

Whatever it meant, Esme did appear to be making an effort to be welcoming. She offered me a barbecue potato chip, then put the bag in the middle of the table so we could all share them.

"I was just starting to tell Esme about what happened with Linda McMuffin," Jenna said. "Want to fill her in?"

"That's okay. You can tell it." I had no interest in reliving the horror story for Esme.

So Jenna got rolling. She added sound effects (the crash of the frame onto the floor, Mom's high-pitched yell at Goober) and vivid descriptions (she said Goober ran off like a bolt of lightning). The way Jenna told it, it didn't sound very much like a horror story. In fact, it actually sounded funny. As I listened to Jenna's telling of it, it occurred to me that the whole thing *was* pretty funny . . . little Goober ruining our big group project with one quick swipe of his paw. Before long, Jenna, Esme, and I were all laughing so hard that I didn't even notice that we had a visitor until Will cleared his throat, loudly.

"*Ahem*. I'm not sure what there is to laugh about when we should be mourning, but I wanted to tell you I have reached a decision."

We stopped laughing and stared up at him.

"Would you like to know what my decision is?"

"Yes, Will." Jenna sounded like she was trying hard to be patient. "Yes, of course we would."

"All right. I have decided that since there is no way we could ever come close to replacing Linda McMuffin, we should go with Ms. Rambutan's second option. We will write a tribute to her in our journal, and then we will have to move on."

"I'm okay with that," Jenna agreed.

Will looked at me. "You know this will mean a point deduction, right, Elfie?"

"Why are you only telling her?" Jenna asked. "It's my grade too."

"Because Elfie worries about grades more than most people do."

I sighed. "It's okay. Believe it or not, I think this is the right decision. We can work on it after school today. Do you guys want to come to my house, since it was supposed to be my turn to take Linda tonight?"

"Yeah . . . why'd you have her last night, anyway?"

"Jenna and I were working together. She was supposed to go home with her afterward."

"Hmm . . . and tragically, that never happened." Will gave us a disapproving look. "Okay, fine. We'll go to your house. Please have good snacks."

He took a barbecue potato chip out of Esme's bag, turned on his heel, and went back to finish lunch with Maxine.

CHAPTER 41

Will seemed happy enough with the snack spread I put out after school: chocolate-covered almonds, mini marshmallows, cheese, crackers, and grapes. He did ask Mom if we had barbecue potato chips, though. "We're fresh out," she said before escaping into the office with her laptop. "Maybe next time." (As far as I knew, Mom had never in her life purchased barbecue potato chips.)

Will was also happy with the journaling supplies Jenna had set up at the kitchen table: stickers, colored pencils, glue sticks, and brightly colored tape for borders.

He was not, however, happy with Goober. Every time he passed through the kitchen, Will glowered at him. But Goober didn't care; in fact, the more Will nudged him away, the more Goober insisted on rubbing against his ankles. He finally gave up.

"Wow, you are persistent," he said after Goober jumped

onto his lap. He looked at him for a second before lifting his hand and scratching him behind his ears. "Well, it's a good thing you're cute; otherwise I'd throw you out into the cold for what you did to Linda."

Without removing Goober from his lap, he took a handful of mini marshmallows and said, "Okay, let's write."

• • •

We worked until right before dinnertime. We decorated the pages that still needed "a little more spark," as Will said. Then we each wrote our own conclusion paragraphs. Will finished his just as his dad arrived to pick him up.

After he put on his jacket in the front hallway, he looked back into the kitchen. "Hey, thanks for all the marshmallows. Want to sit with Maxine and me at lunch again tomorrow?"

I looked at Jenna. She shrugged and nodded, but I wasn't sure if that meant she was okay with it or not.

"What does that mean?" I whispered.

She laughed. "It means do whatever you want, seriously."

I turned back toward Will. "Okay. But I might sit with Jenna and Esme sometimes too."

"Ooh, me too!" he said. "Especially if they have barbecue potato chips." He gave us a deep bow and walked out the front door.

• • •

I was finishing my part of the last journal entry when Uncle Rex arrived to take Jenna home. Mom poked her head out of her office.

"Hey, little brother! Eric is on his way home now; do you and Jenna want to stay for dinner?" Mom came into the kitchen and looked at the snack table. "We're having waffles, probably with some crushed chocolate-covered almonds thrown into the batter."

"Breakfast for dinner at the Osters' again!" Uncle Rex put his arms around Jenna's shoulders. "What do you say, kiddo?"

"Yes, but only if we can put marshmallows into the batter too."

"Fluffy chocolate almond waffles. I like the sound of that. Yeah, Teeney, we'll stay. Thanks."

Mom was taking the waffle iron out of the cabinet when Dad walked in.

"Hey, I spotted the Rex-mobile in the driveway! I hope you guys can stay for dinner."

"Hey, Eric. Yes, Teeney sold us on waffles."

"Excellent. Then you can be here for the big news."

"What big news?" I asked. I had no idea what Dad was talking about. I saw him and Mom trade a quick glance; they knew something I didn't.

"What big news?" I hated not knowing something they knew. "Tell us."

"Okay." Dad sat down at the kitchen table, and Mom joined him. "We finally got an answer from the Hampshire honor code review board today. They emailed Mom and me this afternoon."

"Amazing how quickly it happened after we talked to Colton and his mother," Mom said.

"What did they say?" My stomach felt queasy; suddenly I wasn't sure I wanted Dad to answer me.

"They said they were sorry, and that they made a mistake. Apparently Colton and his parents met with them this morning, and Colton told them the whole story . . . the true version this time."

"So what does that mean?" Jenna asked. "Will they let Elfie back in?"

"They will. As soon as you're ready, Elf; they still have a space for you."

I couldn't believe how quickly my next words came out.

"I'm not ready."

"Well, not right this second, of course." Mom laughed. "But maybe next week?"

"No, I mean I'm not ever going to be ready to go back to Hampshire. I want to stay at Cottonwood."

I'm not sure, but I think I saw Jenna do a tiny fist pump out of the corner of my eye. Uncle Rex was smiling.

Mom and Dad were not.

"What do you mean?" Dad asked. "When did you decide this?"

"I don't know. Recently?"

"How recently?"

"Does it matter?"

"It's just that I thought you were so sure you wanted to go to Hampshire. And we fought for your case, and—"

Mom put her hand on Dad's arm. "I think we're just surprised, Elf," she said. "Can you tell us more about what prompted this decision?"

"I guess I just *like* Cottonwood more now. I actually like it a lot. You might even say I'm *thriving*. I'm in a pretty good class, and I like Ms. Rambutan, and I like lunch, and I even liked our group project."

"You feel comfortable there," Mom suggested.

"Elfie *belongs* there," Jenna chimed in. "It's her school. It's always been her school. We need her there."

"Wow, Jen, that's really nice of you." Uncle Rex could barely hide his shock.

"Well, it's true." She noticed the grown-ups' raised eyebrows and continued. "I know you all have this idea that Elfie and I don't like each other or something, but we get along better than you think. I don't want her to leave."

She looked at me and repeated it. "I don't want you to leave."

I shook my head. "I won't."

Mom looked at Dad. He threw his hands up in the air. "Well, I guess that settles it. What should we do with all that tuition money we'll be saving?"

"I know, I know!" Jenna raised her hand. "Elfie needs a phone."

It was weird. I was starting to get used to agreeing with Jenna.

CHAPTER 42

I had a feeling Mom and Dad would keep asking if I was sure about my decision after Jenna left, and they did. But I was sure. I know Hampshire Academy has a lot of things Cottonwood Elementary never will, like state-of-the-art science equipment and fancy buildings and a gigantic library. But Hampshire will also never have fascinating ants in its cafeteria, or Will and Maxine, or Ms. Rambutan. Or Jenna.

I knew the hardest part was going to be telling Sierra, especially after she went to bat for me with the honor board. But she actually took it pretty well, even though she was disappointed at first.

"Dang it, are you serious?" Those were her first words when I told her about my decision, one day not long afterward when we met at Mugsy's for a pancake lunch.

"I'm sorry," I said. "It was amazing of you to stick up for

me. And I would have liked going to school with you. But I don't really know anyone else there."

"I know; I get it. There are some other kids you'd like, though; we should all hang out sometime. They're nice . . . not snobby like Colton and his crowd. And I really don't get why *he's* being allowed to stay at Hampshire."

"Yeah . . . well, I have a theory about that," I said. I filled Sierra in on the details about Colton's mom. "I never thought I'd say this, but I feel bad for him. And he did eventually tell the truth."

"Wow," Sierra said. "That is tough. Okay, I'll try to give him some latitude. But I'm still not volunteering to be his lab partner anytime soon." She smiled.

"Fair enough."

• • •

Even though I felt good about my decision to stay at Cottonwood, I still have some problems, of course. I know I'll always put pressure on myself to get good grades. But maybe they don't always have to be *perfect* grades. I mean, if I could handle our egg baby crashing to the floor, I think I can handle getting a B. (Okay, okay . . . maybe an A-minus.)

And I know there will always be things I *really* worry about. Like Uncle Rex and Aunt Steph and Jenna . . . and, of course, Rhoda. Sometimes at night I think about her so much that it's hard to fall asleep. When I told Mom that, she sighed and said, "I know. Me too. We both feel help- less. But she knows we're here for her. And sometimes it helps to *do* something . . . maybe we can bake her chocolate turtle brownies to take to her on days when she's not feel- ing sick? Chocolate turtle brownies can be their own kind of medicine."

So we made a plan to bake something for Rhoda to de- liver to her once a week. After our disastrous visit to the hos- pital during her chemo treatment, Mom said we could visit her at home from now on. She knew I was nervous about the possibility of seeing Colton and his mom again; I think she felt the same way. Even though they straightened things out for us at Hampshire, it would still be really awkward to have to spend time with them.

• • •

I wanted to find a way to tell Ms. Rambutan I was doing better than I was when she talked to me about my char- acter study. I wanted her to know she didn't need to worry about me.

I decided to add a P.S. to the final entry in the egg baby journal. I put it on a sticky note so it wouldn't have to stay there forever; this was just between Ms. Rambutan and me.

This is what Will, Jenna, and I wrote:

I have heard grown-ups say that being a parent is like having your heart run around in the world, outside your body. My experience with Linda McMuffin showed me that this is true. Unfortunately, in this case, my heart was also knocked off a bookshelf by a cat. A very, very naughty cat. So my heart was literally broken. But I would still do it all over again, because Linda McMuffin was the best, smartest, most attractive and talented egg baby ever.

—Will Haubner

I learned that babies are a big responsibility. Also that they are extremely fragile, especially if they are eggs. Some parts of having a baby are fun, like choosing their hats and reading them stories. Other parts are really stressful, like figuring out the best way to take care of them, and trying to get your parenting partners to help you and agree with you. At first I wasn't very excited about the egg baby project, but by the end I had fun (even though it had an unhappy ending for our group). If I ever have an egg baby again, I will make sure to keep her close to me, and I won't let her near bookshelves or kittens.

—Jenna Crowe

There is a lot to think about when you have a baby, even if that baby is just an egg. Parents have to think about how to help their babies learn and grow. Of course, most importantly, parents have to keep their babies safe, and I learned the hard way that you should always be mindful of where your baby is, and whether she is in danger.

Like I said, there's a lot to think about when you have a baby. And I learned that parents can get distracted, probably because there is so much to think about in the world in general. For example, this year I have been thinking a lot about my babysitter, Rhoda, who is sick. And how unfair it is that someone so great has to go through something so scary. I've also been thinking a lot about someone in my family who is going through a divorce, and how unfair that is too.

Lately I have also been thinking about something my mom said, that everyone you meet has a story you don't know. And that maybe if we hear each other's stories, we might understand each other more.

Maybe I was thinking about some of these things when I should have been paying better attention to Linda McMuffin. But she was swiped to the floor by my kitten, and now that is part of my story too. (It's the story I'll tell if anyone asks why we didn't get an A+ on this project.)

Hopefully if I ever have an actual baby, I will remember this experience and try not to get too distracted. But I also hope that if I'm ever a real parent to a real human, I will remember that things go wrong no matter how much we plan. Part of being human is learning that it's okay to be unperfect.

—Elfie Oster

And here's what I added for Ms. Rambutan:

Hi Ms. Rambutan—

This note is just from me. I wanted to let you know I don't think group projects are so bad anymore. Even though this one didn't end the way we'd hoped, I had fun.

Also, I know that *unperfect* isn't a word. It's *imperfect*. But I thought you would enjoy the irony of my unperfection.

—Elfie

ACKNOWLEDGMENTS

Creating a book is a serious group project, and I am enormously thankful for the team who helped make it meaningful and fun (this is me being effusive!):

My editor, Nancy Siscoe, whose unceasing enthusiasm and insight added energy, authenticity, and heart to Elfie's world.

Julia Maguire for seeing early potential in this story of a young perfectionist and helping to give it direction.

Sarah Burnes, the most supportive counselor and sounding board.

Dan Santat, whose work I've adored since the day *Beekle* called to me in a bookstore; it was a thrill to see your fantastic rendering of Elfie and her orbit.

Bob Bianchini for his vision and commitment to making books look like friends you'd want to meet.

Copyediting team Artie Bennett, Alison Kolani, Amy Schroeder, and Patricia Callahan for their vigilance in ensuring that every detail meets even Elfie-approved levels of accuracy and precision.

"Critique Pandas" Ariel Bernstein, Ali Bovis, Katie Howes, and Emma Bland Smith; every writer should be lucky enough to have such wise advisers and cheerleaders by their side.

"La Familia Nuclear": Whelan, Lucy, Alice, and Sadie Mahoney. Endless gratitude for making me laugh, having buckets of patience, and keeping life interesting. (Special thanks also to Lucy for naming Linda McMuffin, and to Alice for naming Goober the kitten!)

All the friends and family who support this process and get just as excited about my books as I do.

Finally, to Simon Willis Purchia-McGinn, who recently made me an aunt. Every time our family sees his sweet face, we feel hope. Thank you, Simon, for inspiring us big people to work hard to make the world a little less unperfect.